The Performance of
the Basso Continuo
in Italian Baroque Music

Studies in Musicology, No. 90

George J. Buelow, Series Editor

Professor of Music
Indiana University

Other Titles in This Series

The Performance of the Basso Continuo in Italian Baroque Music

by
Tharald Borgir

 U·M·I Research Press

Ann Arbor, Michigan

Produced and distributed by
UMI Research Press
an imprint of
University Microfilms, Inc.
Ann Arbor, Michigan 48106

Library of Congress Cataloging in Publication Data

Borgir, Tharald.
The performance of the basso continuo in Italian
baroque music.

(Studies in musicology ; no. 90)
Revision of thesis (Ph.D.)—University of California
at Berkeley, 1971.
Bibliography: p.
Includes index.
1. Thorough bass.   2. Music—Italy—17th century—
History and criticism.   I. Title.   II. Series.
ML442.B67   1987   781.3'2'0945   86-25072
ISBN 0-8357-1675-9 (alk. paper)

55,536

Contents

Part Three: The Extended Lutes

Part Four: The Realization of the Continuo Bass

Acknowledgments

The subject of this study was originally suggested by Alan Curtis. An early version of the book owed much to Arthur Hills who helped to clarify and formulate the ideas in a language that is not my mother tongue.

Very little of the original study is included on the following pages; the book in its present form owes its completion to contributions from other people and institutions. The College of Liberal Arts and the Research Office at Oregon State University have provided a series of research grants and assistance in preparing the material for publication. Anita Sullivan read the final draft and made many constructive suggestions. Ronald Jeffers prepared the musical examples; his insights as a composer helped to give greater focus to the illustrations.

Much of the research consisted in surveying large amounts of primary source materials, and in the process I incurred debts of gratitude to many people. The staff at the University of California in Berkeley has always been friendly and helpful, and I am particularly indebted to John Emerson who time and again has gone out of his way to clear up a problem.

Sergio Paganelli, always cordial and interested, gave assistance much beyond the call of duty in my work in the collections at San Petronio and at the Civico Museo Bibliografia Musicale in Bologna. I am also grateful for assistance from the staff at the libraries of the Conservatorio di Musica San Pietro a Maiella in Naples and the Oratorio dei Gerolamini in the same city, at the Conservatorio di Musica Giuseppe Verdi in Milan; further, to the staff at the Biblioteca Nazionale Marciana in Venice, the Biblioteca Estense in Modena, and the British Library in London.

Introduction

The problems of performance to be addressed in this book are all present in Corelli's first collection of church sonatas and are implicit in the title of his opus 1: *Sonate a tre, doi violini, e violone, o arcileuto, col basso per l'organo*. Rome, Mutij, 1681.

The title states that the sonatas are for three instruments, two violins and violone, with the addition of the basso continuo. Today the violone part is regarded as a reinforcement of the basso continuo, yet the title says that violone is one of the three principal instruments. Current notions hold that the doubling of the continuo by the violone always is optional and the instrument may be omitted, yet Corelli's title suggests that its importance is on a par with the two violin parts. Is this simply a matter of semantics, or are our notions about bass-line doubling in need of revision? The first and largest part of the book addresses this question.

The bass instrument mentioned first is the violone, an instrument often thought to be a double bass. The contrapuntal nature of the bass part strongly suggests that it needs to be played at notated pitch, not one octave below. At the heart of this matter is the Italian use of the term *violone* to refer to a number of different instruments. The problems of terminology cannot be adequately dealt with without reviewing all the bowed bass instruments of the period. Such a review forms the second part of the book.

Corelli's title indicates that the bass part can be played by a violone *or* an archlute, an option very common in church sonatas from that time. The archlute is generally considered to be a chordal instrument used for the realization of the continuo. Since the bass part is thought of as a doubling of the continuo, it seems logical that the archlute would play a realization in addition to that on the organ. But the archlute in this work is mentioned as a substitute for an instrument playing a single contrapuntal line. Was the part played differently by the two instruments, as a single line by the violone and as a realization by the archlute? The question simply points out how little is known about the archlute, and of the extended lutes in general. These instruments were employed in practically all genres of Italian music from the seventeenth century, and in order to understand basso continuo practice it is essential to know something more about their use. The extended lutes will be the subject of the third part of this book.

Important as these various issues may be, the core of basso continuo practice is ultimately the realization of the bass line. The subject has been dealt with extensively in the standard literature, yet a number of important Italian sources have been overlooked. Moreover, the improvisation of keyboard solos from a bass, a significant aspect of Italian continuo practice, is hardly known at all. The realization of the bass, in the accompaniment or in keyboard solos, is the subject of the fourth and last part of this book.

Part One

Bass-Line Doubling in
Italian Baroque Music

1

Bass-Line Doubling in
Italian Baroque Music: A Practice Yet
to Be Justified

The Case for Bass-Line Doubling Reviewed

One of the basic tenets of basso continuo practice, as understood in the twentieth century, is that two instruments are needed for its proper performance: a chordal instrument for the realization, and a cello or viola da gamba to sustain and reinforce the bass line. This view is taken for granted in practically all writings on the subject and is found in all major dictionaries, in books on music history, in texts for music appreciation classes, etc. Modern editions of baroque music routinely include a part for a bass-line instrument even when such a part was not included in the original performance material. Performers, whether interested in authenticity or not, follow the same practice as editors. Nevertheless, the automatic inclusion of bass-line instruments in seventeenth-century music is based on the flimsiest evidence, and their use in the eighteenth century may have been more limited than one is led to believe.

The rationale for including a bass-line instrument comes from two kinds of sources: (1) statements in the theoretical literature, and (2) the presence of instrumental bass parts in addition to the basso continuo in the original performance material. The extra bass parts, however, are found in some genres and not in others. Considering the whole range of seventeenth-century music, their presence cannot be taken as evidence for a general practice of bass-line doubling. More importantly, the theoretical evidence is suspect, to say the least. Only two baroque sources unequivocally recommend doubling. Best known is the following passage from C.P.E. Bach's treatise on keyboard performance: "The Most complete accompaniment to a Solo, to which nobody can take an exception, is a keyed instrument in conjunction with the Violoncello (Arnold 1931, 237) [Das vollkommenste

Accompagnement beim Solo, da wider niemand etwas einwenden kann, ist ein Clavierinstrument nebst dem Violoncell (1762, vol.2: Introduction, 9)].

The statement concerns solos only, not ensemble music or orchestral music. Considering the exactitude of C.P.E. Bach's writing in general, it is doubtful whether the statement has implications beyond the situation to' which it is addressed; yet, it has been the cornerstone for the practice of doubling the bass line in all types of music.

The other eighteenth-century source recommending bass-line doubling is the preface to François Couperin's *Leçons de ténèbres* (1714). The composer suggests that it is desirable to add a bass viol or a cello to the chordal instrument, but the participation is clearly optional. Also, the context here is that of a solo, and the recommendation for doubling is tentative.

These statements, limited in scope as they are, have been taken as proof of a general practice of bass-line doubling in the eighteenth century. They also form the basis on which this practice has been projected backwards so that the writings of seventeenth-century theorists are interpreted as if bass-line doubling were an established fact in their time. Their statements, when scrutinized, do not support such an interpretation. Most of the relevant seventeenth-century sources are referred to in the following summation taken from an article on organ continuo by Peter Williams (1969, 148): " 'Add a trombone where possible if the organetto is small' (Agazzari 1607) or a bassoon or dulzian (Praetorius 1619, p. 145) instead of the violone (Agazzari 1608) or 'chitarrone or a bassoon or any other instrument that can play quickly' in the *Messa concertata* of Cavalli's 'Musiche Sacre' (Venice, 1656)." The brevity of the references is indicative of the generally held view that bass-line doubling is not a matter of dispute and that extensive documentation is unnecessary. The first part of the quotation is paraphrased from Agazzari's treatise *Del sonare sopra il basso* (1607), and in the original text the passage goes as follows: "And sometimes the trombone in small ensembles is used as *contrabasso* when the *organetti* are one octave above [notated pitch] [E tal volta il trombone in picciol conserto, s'adopera per contrabasso, quando sono organetti all'ottave alta] ([1607] Kinkeldey 1910, 216)."

The reference occurs in a discussion of wind instruments, for which Agazzari had little use. When the organ plays an octave above normal pitch the trombone plays the bass part one octave lower. This is not really a case of bass-line doubling but is merely a way of supplying the real bass when the chordal instrument is a four-foot organ.

The quotation from Cavalli's *Musiche sacre* is found in a printer's note which explains that the violoncello part may be played by an archlute, a bassoon or other similar instrument, or that it may be left out altogether. The important point is that the cello is part of an instrumental trio which includes two violins. The three instruments invariably play together as a group. In the vocal sections, which constitute by far the larger part of the work, the cello participates only if the violins also play. Since the string trio participates only intermittently, the basso continuo is mostly played by the organ alone. And since the cello part is optional, the doubling of the bass is not considered necessary even in the instrumental sections. Far from being proof of bass-line doubling, the performance indications in the *Musiche sacre* argue against it.

The most frequently quoted source on seventeenth-century bass-line doubling is Michael Praetorius's *Syntagma musicum* (1619b, vol. 3). Large sections of the third volume are devoted to figured bass practice, and the comments on bass-line doubling constitute part of the advice to fledgling organists:

> It is also particularly to be observed, when 2 or 3 [solo] voices sing to the accompaniment of the General Bass which the Organist or Lutenist has before him and plays from, that it is very good, indeed almost necessary, to have the same General Bass played, in addition, by some bass instrument, such as a Bassoon, Dulcian, or Trombone, or, what is best of all, on a Violone. I have therefore exhorted several singers, that a number of them should (as would be very praiseworthy) practice playing the Bass Viol in the chorus, which is a very easy matter, and is an admirable adornment to the foundation, and helps to strengthen it, since one cannot, in every school, always have good bass singers.
>
> Or one can also have the General Bass sung, to which end I have added the words, as well as they could be adapted, in those *Cantiones* in which the words are not already to be found in the instrumental Basses. (Arnold 1931, 99)

> [Ist diss auch sonderlich zu mercken, Wenn 2. oder 3 Stimmen allein in den *General Bass*, denn der Organist, oder Lauttenist für sich hat, and draus schlagt, gesungen werden; Dass es sehr gut, auch fast notig sey, denselben *General Bass* mit einem *Bass Instrument*, als Fagott, Dolcian oder Posaun, oder aber, welchs zum allerbesten, mit einer Bassgeigen, darzu machen lest. Darum ich dann etliche *Cantores* darzu ermahnet, und wer sehrzu loben, wenn es ihrer viel also for die hand nehmen, dass sie sich off einer Bassgeigen, den Bass im Chor mitzustreichen, (welches dann gar eine leichte kunst ist) *execiren* mochten, welches, weil man in allen Schulen nicht allezeit gute Bassisten haben kann, das Fundament trefflich zieret und stercken hilfft.
>
> Oder man kan auch den *General Bass* darzu singen lassen, darum ich dann Text so gut er sich darzu schicken wollen, darunter applicirt, in denen Cantonibus, wo der Text nich allbereit in den *Instrumental* Bassen zu finden seyn wird. (Praetorius 1619b, 3:145)]

Thus, a bowed bass instrument may be added under two different circumstances. Choir members may simply play along for the purpose of practicing the instrument, the performance benefiting from such practicing because bass singers are in short supply. The musical purpose for including the cello is not to strengthen the bass per se, but to provide support when the vocal bass part is undermanned.

The second and more important situation, described at the beginning of the quotation, refers to music for two or three solo singers. The limitations are important: Praetorius is not concerned with solos, quartets, or choral music. The option of having the General Bass sung rather than played suggests that the ensemble excludes the bass. The problem appears to be balance: with two or three high voices the ensemble was "top-heavy" and needed strengthening in the bass. With four voices a bass would be included, and solos have a sufficiently light texture for the basso continuo to hold its own.

The limited application of Praetorius's remarks is apparent when considered in the context of the third part of the *Syntagma musicum*. The above quotation occurs in a section that describes twenty different ways of combining voices and instruments in the performance of sacred vocal music. None of the remaining nineteen mention bass-line doubling (Praetorius 1619b, 3:169–98).

In the *Polyhymnia caduceatrix & panegyrica,* also from 1619, Praetorius demonstrates the application of the twenty ways of combining voices and instruments described in the *Syntagma*. Apart from the larger ensembles which optionally may be performed with fewer voices, there are only three pieces in two or three parts. In two of these pieces the upper parts call for both voice and instrument so that the instrumental doubling of the bass is offset by a similar doubling in the treble register.

The discussion in *Syntagma* and the music of the *Polyhymnia* show Praetorius as a proponent of the renaissance practice of freely mixing voices and instruments. Being incidental results of such mixing, the examples of bass-line doubling are not indicative of an accepted practice, nor can they be taken as a guideline for the future.

Procedure

Given the twentieth-century custom of considering a bass-line instrument a necessary part of the basso continuo, it is quite remarkable that documentation of such a practice is lacking. The support for bass-line doubling comes from countries other than Italy and from the eighteenth century (C. P. E. Bach, 1762). Seventeenth-century sources are often quite explicit on the performance of the continuo, yet they fail to give any general advice on the inclusion of bass instruments. Studying the question of doubling of the basso continuo in Italian music, therefore, starts without any documentation that such a practice ever existed.

Many kinds of sources will have to be considered in this study. The theoretical literature, though already scrutinized by several generations of scholars, may still yield some useful information. Payment records are important in documenting what kinds of players were available at a given place and time, and for special performances. Descriptions of performances may be very useful but only rarely do they contain the kind of details needed to assess instrumental usage.

The most promising source material is music from the time considered in conjunction with original performance material. Scores are rare except in opera and oratorio; they are often sketchy and rarely reveal much of interest about the continuo. Most baroque music survives in sets of performing parts, and these are important in showing which instruments were included. The bass-line player may of course have read from the part for the chordal instrument. Such a practice, however, would need to be documented; the possibility that two players *can* read from the same part is not in itself proof that it actually took place.

Even a superficial examination of the source material suggests that parts for bass-line instruments were included in some types of music and not in others. It will therefore be necessary to focus on the principal genres to see how performance traditions differed and to observe how changes in style may have influenced performances. The following categories seem most useful for the present purposes: secular vocal music, sacred vocal music, secular instrumental music, sacred instrumental music, and large-scale dramatic works. Each of these will be dealt with in a separate chapter.

Several of the genres of the baroque period have their roots in sixteenth-century music. Many musical forms evolved from predecessors in the renaissance, and the original performance requirements may have had a bearing upon seventeenth-century usage. It is therefore necessary to start with an assessment of what kinds of accompaniments, if any, may have been practiced in the sixteenth century.

2

The Origin of the Basso Continuo

The Emergence of the Basso Continuo

The emergence of the basso continuo is intimately tied to the stylistic revolution that marked the beginning of the baroque period in music. The ensemble music of the renaissance, usually in four or more parts, disappeared and was supplanted by works in which one or a few solo performers are supported by a simple accompaniment played on a chordal instrument. New genres arose, such as the vocal monody, and old genres were transformed, as in the case of the *canzona da sonare* which, under the influence of the basso continuo, changed into the church sonata. Within a short time the continuo became ubiquitous, a fact that caused Hugo Riemann to coin the term *Generalbasszeitalter* — the age of thoroughbass — to describe what today generally is called the baroque era.

The first printed basso continuo part appeared in a polychoral work by Giovanni Croce, *Motetti a otto voci*, published in Venice in 1594. A sprinkling of such parts is found in sacred choral compositions in the following years, but the watershed was reached in 1600. That year saw the appearance of the first works in the new style. Large-scale dramatic works featuring the new recitative style were introduced in Giulio Caccini's opera *Euridice* (1600) and its religious counterpart, Emilio de'Cavalieri's *La Rappresentatione di anima e di corpo* (1600). The secular solo song, though having deep roots in the sixteenth century, was brought into prominence with Caccini's *Nuove musiche* (1601) and soon supplanted the multipart madrigal. The following year saw the appearance of Viadana's *Cento concerti* (1602) which established sacred monody as an important genre. Instrumental ensemble music, as yet of relatively little importance in Italian music, was affected more slowly by the basso continuo, and the full effect did not show up until the 1620s.

The monodic publications by Caccini and Viadana, mentioned above, both contain prefaces with important commentary on the basso continuo. A most significant document for the understanding of the musical practice in this transitional period is Agazzari's *Del sonare sopra il basso con tutti instrumenti* (1607). He was primarily concerned with the performance of sacred music and his often-quoted distinction between ornamenting instruments and foundation instruments—those realizing the bass—reflects the practice of the past more than that of the future.

During the following few years a number of other musicians discussed the continuo: Bianciardi (1607), Diruta (1609), and Banchieri (1611). The writings of Praetorius (1619b) are also important in that he had first-hand knowledge of Italian practice and often referred to Italian sources.

Terminology

The expression "basso continuo" is only one of a number of terms used around 1600 to refer to the accompaniment. The following list shows the most important ones in the order in which they appeared in publications.

spartitura	1594, Venice. G. Croce: *Spartitura delli motetti a otto voci.*
partidura	1596, Venice. G. Croce: *Messe a otto voci.*
partitio	1598, Milan. J. Gallus: *Sacri operis musici alternis modulis concinendi.*
basso principale	1598, Milan. Orfeo Vecchi: *Basso principale da sonare delli salmi intieri a cinque voci.*
basso per l'organo	1599, Milan. G. Bassano: *Motetti per concerti ecclesiastici.*
parte de i bassi	1599, Venice. *Motetti e salmi a otto voci . . . otto eccel. Autori.*
basso continuato	1600, Rome. E. de' Cavalieri: *Rappresentatione di anima e di corpo.*
basso generale	1600, Venice. G. Fattorini: *Sacri concertia due voci . . .*
gravium partium	1602, Venice. G. Zucchini: *Harmonia Sacra.*
basso continuo	1602, Venice. L. Grosso da Viadana: *Cento concerti ecclesiastici.*
partimento	1605, Venice. G.M. Trabaci: *Missarum, et motectorum quatuor vocum.*
basso seguente	1607, Venice. A. Banchieri: *Ecclesiastiche sinfonie.*

| *basso seguito* | 1610, Venice. G. Piccioni: *Concerti ecclesiastici.* |
| *partitione* | 1616, Naples. M. Trabaci: *Missarum, liber primus, cum partitione organi noviter impressa.* |

Some of the terms have remained in our vocabulary, some have changed meaning, and at least one important term has gone unnoticed.

Basso Continuo

The origin of this term is frequently associated with the accompaniment of vocal polyphony in which the lowest notes in the texture were extracted so as to form a continuous bass line, hence, basso continuo. The argument is logical but not persuasive: the term is first found in Viadana's concertos, many of which are for a single voice with accompaniment so that the bass is an independent and essential part. Basso continuo became the standard term in northern Italy; the equivalent term in southern Italy appears to have been *partimento* (see below).

Basso per L'Organo, Parte de i Bassi, Gravium Partium

All these expressions imply that the accompaniment is played from a bass part. Later on the word "basso" alone is commonly used in the same sense. When found in titles and part books, basso refers to a chordal instrument, rarely to a bass-line instrument, which normally would be mentioned by name.

Basso Seguente

Today's dictionary definition, erroneous in terms of seventeenth-century usage, ties this term to a continuo part that duplicates the lowest vocal part throughout the composition. However, Banchieri, who introduced the term, treats it as a synonym for basso continuo. In his *Gemelli armonici* (1609b) the organ part is marked "basso continuo" while the preface repeatedly refers to it as the "basso seguente." Since the part is independent of the two upper voices it would not qualify as a *basso seguente* as that term is understood today. As an alternative to the modern use of *basso seguente* one might consider "dependent bass" which will be used below.

Spartidura, Partitura, Partitio, Partitione, Partimento

Derived from the verb [s]*partire*—to divide—these terms refer to the verti-
cal lines that align the parts in a score, similar to bar lines. The barring is
applied inconsistently and may be found in only a few pieces. These terms
quickly went out of use for continuo parts save one, *partimento,* which in
southern Italy became the standard term for thoroughbass. It is found in
publications (Nenna 1622, Montalbano 1629), including one theoretical
treatise (Cavaliere 1634), and is ubiquitous in the rich seventeenth-century
manuscript collection at the Oratorio dei Gerolamini in Naples. This usage,
which continues into the eighteenth century, has gone unnoticed, with the
result that some of the most interesting sources on eighteenth century continuo practice have remained completely unknown: the partimenti by early
eighteenth-century Neapolitan theorists and composers. These will be fully
explored in part four.

The Sixteenth-Century Roots of the Basso Continuo

Our notion of the emergence of thoroughbass is shaped by documentary
evidence: continuo parts, prefaces, and treatises. These do not mark the
beginning but, rather, the surfacing of a practice that had been in existence
for some time. The earliest printed basso continuo parts, appearing in the
1590s, fail to explain how to make a realization, this skill being taken for
granted. These parts satisfied an existing need. As mentioned in prefaces
and titles, they were included for the convenience of the organist who
otherwise had to make one up.

The use of chordal instruments for accompaniment in the sixteenth
century is poorly documented except in one case: the Florentine *Intermedii*
(Brown 1973). These represent a local tradition, but may well also reflect
general trends in the development of instrumentation in other repertories.

While the earlier *Intermedii* feature consort instrumentation, those
from the middle of the sixteenth century onward increasingly mix various
kinds of instruments and voices. Included in these mixed ensembles are
plucked instruments, primarily lutes and harpsichords. These "foundation
instruments" may originally have been intended to double the vocal parts
but were increasingly used for a freer accompaniment of the kind that we
now would think of as a continuo realization (Brown 1973, 78).

Secular songs were occasionally performed as solos in the sixteenth
century, and indications are that the accompaniment often consisted of an
intabulation of the complete piece for a chordal instrument (Brown 1973,
23). This is true, for instance, of the intabulations included in Ortiz's *Tratado* (1553). But Ortiz also includes a number of instrumental pieces in

which only the bass part is given, and since he does not include any explanations of how to make the realization, he must have counted on the performer to have the necessary skills to do so. A performer who possessed this skill, if confronted with the task of providing a keyboard part for one of the large ensembles in the *Intermedii,* must have been sorely tempted to play a realization rather than go through the cumbersome task of preparing a full score.

Ortiz's use of unfigured basses raises the question of whether something approaching figured bass playing may have been practiced as early as the middle of the sixteenth century. Instrumental ensemble music of that time may, in fact, call for such accompaniment. The earliest known publication in this genre is the *Musica nova,* which appeared in 1540. The title bears a suggestive similarity to those of later works that include a basso continuo or deal with that subject: *Musica nova. Accomodate per cantar et sonar sopra organi; et altri strumenti* (Venice, 1540).

The mention of the organ in the *Musica nova* is generally taken to mean that the contents may be sung, or played on the organ, or played by other instruments (Slim 1964, 1:xxxvii). Playing the pieces on the organ would require a score that the player had to write out. The existence of a few sixteenth-century scores suggests that such a procedure may have been followed (Slim 1964, 1:xxxvii). But given the difficulty of reading from an open score, the extra work in making it up, and the fact that the *Musica nova* was published in parts suggest solo organ performance to have been the exception rather than the rule. Organ participation may rather have been in the form of accompaniment. The title literally states that the contents are "to be sung and played above organs." In other words, the organ participated whether the parts were sung or played. The expression "cantar et sonar sopra organi," used in *Musica nova,* is very similar to the expression "cantare e sonare sopra il basso," used around 1600, which refers to solo parts played above a basso continuo, as in the case of A. Banchieri's *Ecclesiastiche sinfonie dette canzoni in aria francese a quattro voci, per sonare, e cantare, & sopra un basso seguente concertare entro Organo* (Venice, 1607).

Both titles speak of singing and playing, and both mention the organ. Banchieri speaks in terms of the part serving the organist, the basso seguente; the *Musica nova* speaks of the specific instrument, the organ. In either case the intention seems to be for the keyboard instrument to provide a realization.

Titles similar to that of the *Musica nova* are common in instrumental as well as vocal music from the mid-sixteenth century (Slim 1964, 1:xxxvii). Reese (1959, 529, 537) observes that some of the instrumental works were published simultaneously in organ tablature, from which he concludes that ensemble performance must have been the primary purpose of the part-book edition. His argument further strengthens the case for considering the reference to the organ in the ensemble versions to imply accompaniment and not solo performance.

Basso Continuo Parts in Sacred Vocal Music

In considering the sixteenth-century roots of the basso continuo, two areas are of special importance: sacred music, and secular solo song. In these areas one finds direct links between renaissance and baroque performance practice, links that are important for assessing the degree to which past practices were carried into the seventeenth century.

Sacred polyphony in the sixteenth century, like the music of the Florentine *Intermedii*, was performed with a mixture of voices and instruments. Though the publications of sacred music mention only voices, the inclusion of instruments was so common that purely vocal renditions may have been the exception rather than the rule (Abraham 1968, 4:522). Exactly how the instruments participated is not known and probably varied a great deal depending on the place, time, and circumstances. Since the music was published in parts, one can envision a purely instrumental rendition of some or all of the parts, or instrumental doubling of vocal lines. At times a single keyboard instrument might take care of the doubling of all the parts. That, however, would require the organist to make a keyboard score from the parts. This time-consuming task could have been carried out only occasionally; Agazzari ([1607] Kinkeldey 1910, 221) points out that if the organist were to make scores for every piece used in the service, he would in one year end up with a larger library than a doctor of law.

Everything considered, it seems likely that organists practiced some kind of simplified accompaniment for decades before the first basso continuo parts appeared in print (Croce 1594). Viadana ([1602] Arnold 1931, 20) and Agazzari ([1607] Kinkeldey 1910, 221) both point out that not every organist was capable of reading a keyboard score at sight. But even with only a rudimentary understanding of chords, the organist had an easy recourse in the vocal bass part which, with a few emendations, could serve as a continuo part. The difficulties came in polychoral works where neither of the two (or more) bass parts provided a satisfactory basis for the accompaniment. It is hardly coincidence that the first printed continuo part occurs in a polychoral work (Croce 1594). But while these parts served a real need they also gave the organists a taste of the convenience of a ready-made part. Such parts were soon included in music for a single choir as well and within a short time became standard in publications of sacred polyphony.

The problem of whether to accompany from a keyboard score or to improvise a realization from a bass was still an issue in the early seventeenth century. Given the general practice of duplicating the parts with single-line instruments, it is hardly surprising that several authorities prefer that the organ do the same. Diruta (1609, Libro 4, p. 16) dismisses continuo accompaniment as inadequate, and even Viadana ([1602] Arnold 1931, 20), one of the champions of the new style, concedes that a keyboard score is the best solution. But Viadana also points out that the continuo is easier to play, and this was the prevailing opinion.

Nevertheless, the early continuo parts clearly illustrate an ambivalence regarding the proper nature of the accompaniment for sacred polyphony. The published parts show a great deal of variety: full scores, short scores of several kinds, and single-line basso continuo parts (Horsley 1977). Two or more of these may be contained in the same publication. The short scores provide insights on the changing ideal of the accompaniment. Some scores include only the two outer parts, a solution unacceptable in terms of later injunctions against doubling the highest line. In terms of renaissance practice, however, the procedure is perfectly logical: instead of doubling all the parts the organ plays only the most important ones, the soprano and the bass. But practical considerations also played a role: Banchieri (1609a, 24) points out that the inclusion of the upper part is a great help in finding the chords.

Another type of score also contains the bass and soprano but adds a composite third part showing the fugal entries of the other voices. This special feature is adopted in later basso continuo parts so that imitative entries are shown in their proper register, one after the other. Such sections, notated in the clefs of the imitative parts as they enter, became known as *bassetti*.

In the end the various types of scores proved too cumbersome for the new age and disappeared by about 1620. Sacred music from then on contained a single-line basso continuo part.

The organ part was intended for that instrument alone. The use of the organ very likely grew out of the general practice of mixing voices and instruments. Instead of having single-line instruments reinforcing each of the parts, the organ alone took care of them all. There was no particular concern for strengthening any single part, and that is of course true of the bass as well.

Secular Monody

Within a decade of its first appearance in print monody dominated the field of secular vocal music. This dramatic rise in popularity tends to overshadow the fact that solo singing had deep roots in the past. Describing the new style, Caccini, in *Nuove musiche* ([1601] Strunk 1950, 379) speaks about the novelty in terms of the affective performance, not in terms of the texture. He and countless others had been singing solos to a chordal accompaniment for a long time.

The lute song was popular throughout the sixteenth century, and *frottole, villanelle,* and *canzonette* were performed both as solos with accompaniment and as part-songs (Abraham 1968, 4:143). Toward the end of the century Caccini describes how polyphonic madrigals were also performed as solos to the accompaniment of a lute ([1601] Strunk 1950, 379).

As suggested by the expression "lute-song," the accompaniment was performed by a single instrument, and several accounts testify to that effect. Describing the stylistic changes in the 1570s, Giustiniani ([1628] 1878, 15) says they were "particularly noticeable in performances by *solo voice and one instrument*" (author's translation, italics added). The idea that the accompaniment was carried out by a single instrument is corroborated by Caccini. In describing the performance of a monody—he calls it a solo madrigal—he reports that the audience "had never before heard harmony of *a single voice, accompanied by a single instrument* with such power to move the passion of the mind" (italics added) ([1601] Strunk 1950, 379).

The principal reason for preferring one instrument only for the accompaniment is to preserve the freedom of the soloist, which is the essence of the new style. Ideally, the singer should also be the accompanist: Caccini recommends that one "sing to a theorbo or other stringed instrument" to avoid "being compelled to fit himself to others" ([1601] Strunk 1950, 391). A single instrument suffices, and the inclusion of any more than that would inhibit the performer. This attitude carried over to the literal flood of monodies that appeared during the first decades of the seventeenth century. Nigel Fortune's study of this repertory (1953) fails to identify a single indication for using a bass-line instrument in addition to the one realizing the bass. Fortune is the first scholar to seriously question the notion that bass-line doubling should take place as a matter of course. Within the repertory he discusses, secular Italian song up to about 1640, there are no indications that the basso continuo was doubled, nor is there any hint that such a practice was tacitly carried over from the sixteenth century.

Sacred Monody

While secular monody has deep roots in the renaissance, sacred monody is a product of the stylistic ferment at the end of the sixteenth century. Viadana, like Caccini, describes the performance of vocal polyphony by solo voice and accompaniment. Unlike Caccini's "modern madrigals" which are for a single voice and accompaniment, Viadana's sacred concertos also include duets, in all conceivable combinations of voice ranges, and assorted pieces in three and four parts.

The subordinate role of the organ is reflected in the table of contents and in the contrapuntal nature of the parts. In the table the pieces are listed according to the number of voices, excluding the basso continuo. A *concerto a uno* is performed by one singer and organ, a *concerto a due* by two singers and organ, and so on. More important, the subordinate role of the organ is reflected in the nature of its part. In the solo concertos all the musical interest is concentrated in the vocal line, and the basso continuo features only slow motion. Similarly, in the other concertos the melodically significant material is the exclusive domain of the voices. When one of the vocal parts is a bass it may seem that the basso continuo is of melodic importance since the two parts are often identical. But the appearance is deceptive because the table, as we have seen, identifies the voices as the principal parts and the organ as a subordinate adjunct. Indeed, the organ part is often simplified by the removal of animated motion, thereby reducing the part to the harmonically significant notes needed for the realization.

Summary

The review of the birth of the basso continuo practice and its roots in sixteenth-century music fails to provide any argument for doubling the bass line. Theorists make no statements in support of a such a practice. The discussions by Viadana, Agazzari, Diruta, Banchieri, and Praetorius provide ample opportunities for discussion of the subject of doubling, yet none occurs. When early seventeenth-century composers, in treatises and prefaces, speak of the basso continuo with reference only to a chordal instrument, the implication is that no other instrument was needed or desirable.

The view of the theorists is corroborated in the music of the time. In the early seventeenth century, vocal music contains a single continuo part and no instrumental reinforcement of the bass. The continuo was the domain of the chordal instrument alone in sacred as well as in secular music. And the spirit of secular monody demanded a flexible accompaniment best provided by a single performer, preferably the vocal soloist. In short, the theorists, the performing traditions, the music, and the publications provide no support for the view that a general practice of bass-line doubling existed at the beginning of the baroque period.

Confronted with a work having similar bass and basso continuo parts, a modern observer is apt to see quite different implications than a seventeenth-century musician. Looking at Viadana's *Sacred Concertos*, the modern observer would perceive the basso continuo as a principal part doubled by the vocal bass. For Viadana *the vocal bass was the principal part, doubled by the dependent basso continuo.*

Viadana's view of the relationship between the bass continuo and the bass part is exactly the opposite of the prevailing view in our days. His view, shared by his Italian contemporaries and applicable to instrumental music as well as vocal music, provides a new perspective on the question of doubling of the basso continuo that will be further explored on the following pages.

3

The Church Sonata

The So-Called Trio Sonata

Though the baroque period is one dominated by vocal music, the instrumental music of the period is much better known today. The most important genre is the so-called trio sonata, a work for two treble instruments and basso continuo. The bass-line instrument, when included, is seen as a concertante part that elaborates the basso continuo (Newman 1983, 51). This generally accepted view has obscured the true function of the bass part and the contrapuntal nature of works in this genre.

Implicit in this view is the notion that "baroque titles are no sure clue to either the number of separate parts or the number of players intended" (Newman 1983, 52). The statement is necessarily true if one assumes that the continuo is doubled whether a part for the bass-line instrument is included or not; it is also true when music from the baroque is considered without allowing for national differences. But it is not true in Italy where titles of instrumental sonatas are reliable guides to the number of instruments the composer considered necessary.*

The expression "trio sonata" includes both the chamber sonata and the church sonata. The similarity of the textures has tended to eclipse the substantial differences between the two kinds of works. Publications of chamber sonatas frequently had three parts, two violins and bass, while church sonatas generally had four, two violins, bass, and basso continuo. The difference was easily explained on the assumption that the continuo of the chamber sonata should be performed by two players. Once this faulty assumption has been removed, the way is open for the realization that the

---

* N. M. Jensen's work on the the instrumental music of the late seventeenth century parallels the author's work with the same repertory. Unaware of the efforts of the other, we both arrived at similar conclusions. Jensen published his results in the Larsen Festschrift in 1972; the author's results were included in his doctoral dissertation at University of California at Berkeley in 1971.

two genres have completely different performance traditions and that chamber sonatas were frequently rendered without a basso continuo.

In order for these performance traditions to be understood, the two genres need to be studied separately. The church sonata is the natural starting point. The frequent inclusion of a separate bass part in addition to the basso continuo provides an opportunity to examine the need for such parts, a point of central importance in this study.

The two kinds of sonatas took shape after 1650. Publications from the earlier part of the century frequently contain a confusing array of works. Titles such as canzona, sonata, capriccio, sinfonia, and the like are used for pieces of an essentially similar nature. It is questionable whether the composers themselves distinguished between these terms in ways that correspond to our systems of classification. The term "sonata" for example, does not refer to twentieth-century categories such as form and genre, but to pieces that were played rather than sung.

Distinctions within this repertory must be made on stylistic grounds. A substantial segment of early seventeenth-century instrumental ensemble music is of contrapuntal nature and of a structure that points back to the *canzona da sonare*. The canzona was used in the church service, and it is therefore not surprising that its developments lead directly to the church sonata, which had a similar function.

The Canzona

Published basso continuo parts appeared somewhat later in instrumental music than in vocal music, the earliest known example being Antonio Troilo's *Canzoni da suonare* from 1606. As in vocal polyphony, the basso continuo was added to pieces that in themselves were complete. The titles customarily indicated the number of the parts; in the case of Troilo's canzonas, four and five. The continuo was not counted among the principal parts; a *canzona a quattro* employed four single-line instruments plus the organ.

The basso continuo created opportunities for textural changes in the canzona similar to those introduced in vocal music by Viadana. Since the accompaniment took over some of the function of the inner parts, namely, that of filling out the harmony, the number of contrapuntal parts could be reduced. The earliest examples of this kind appeared in 1610 in a collection of sacred (vocal) concertos by Paolo Cima. The work contains six instrumental pieces with from two to four parts, four sonatas by Cima himself, and two capriccios by his brother, Andrea. These pieces, which all include an independent bass, are in the table of contents identified according to the number of contrapuntal parts. The basso continuo, which by and large

Table 1.1.   Listing of Contents of G. Frescobaldi,
Il primo libro delle canzoni

> *Canto solo* (4 canzonas)
> *Basso solo* (4)
> *A due canti* (5)
> *A due bassi* (4)
> *Canto e basso* (6)
> *A tre, due bassi e canto* (3)
> [*A tre,*] *due canti, e basso* (3)
> *A quattro, due canti e due bassi* (5)
> [*A quattro,*] *canto, alto, tenor, e basso* (3)

doubles the bass, is not counted among the principal parts in the table of contents. A *sonata a due* is for three instruments, two playing the principal parts, and a chordal instrument playing basso continuo.

Instrumental ensemble pieces like those by the Cimas continued to appear in collections of vocal music in the following decade, but by 1620 the new genre had caught on to the point that publications with only instrumental pieces started to appear. Like Viadana's sacred concertos, the collections of modified canzonas contained a great variety of textures and tessituras. One of the first such works is Frescobaldi's *Il primo libro delle canzoni, ad una, due, tre e quattro voci,* published in Rome in 1623, and reissued several times with additions and alterations. The five printed parts are marked *Canto I, Canto II, Basso I, Basso II,* and *basso generale.* A summary of the contents of the 1628 edition in table 1.1 shows the disposition of the textures.

The pieces are predominantly for treble and bass instruments; only the four-part pieces contain parts in the alto and tenor ranges. As in Cima's sonatas, the basso continuo, though indispensable in most of the pieces, is not counted among the principal parts. The principal parts, which are listed in the table, are always imitative and often rhythmically animated. By contrast, the slowly-moving basso continuo is devoid of intrinsic interest. Thus a canzona for two trebles focuses the activity in the upper parts. In those for treble and bass the two parts engage in imitations while the basso continuo, a simplified version of the bass, is much like the corresponding part in the pieces for two trebles. Whenever one of the principal parts is a bass, the basso continuo is similarly simplified. This is true even in the pieces for solo bass, which thus have only one real part. In short, the continuo part is stripped of ornamental motion and reduced to the harmonically active notes.

All the Frescobaldi canzonas, save those for solo treble, feature a subordinate basso continuo. The solo treble pieces are anomalies in terms of early seventeenth-century practices and traditions. The canzona is characterized by its contrapuntal texture and the use of imitations. In works for a single instrument these central traits must by necessity be omitted. Frescobaldi circumvented the problem by including the imitations in the organ part. In doing so he in effect turned the pieces into *canzoni a due* for treble and (organ) bass. The solution is incompatible with contemporary notions of the relationship between the principal parts and the basso continuo. A *solo canzona*, because of the absence of counterpoint and imitations, is a contradiction in terms. That is probably the reason why a solo repertory did not develop within this genre for a long time. Significantly, when Corelli wrote solo sonatas for violin at the end of the century, those in the canzona tradition included extensive use of double stops to maintain the contrapuntal quality of the texture.

The baroque version of the canzona, the *sonata da chiesa*, maintained the imitative counterpoint of its ancestor, but abandoned the four- and five-part textures as the continuo took over the function of the inner parts. Solo canzonas did not develop for the reasons just described. The vast majority of church sonatas, therefore, have two or three principal parts.

The Church Sonata

The two- and three-part works within the canzona tradition, first found in the 1620s, had by the middle of the century become the prevailing form within this genre. Publications of such works were increasingly entitled *sonate* with or without the qualifier *da chiesa*. After about 1650 the continuo instrument was always the organ. Sartori's bibliography of Italian instrumental music (1952) contains no examples of church sonatas accompanied by harpsichord, and the use of the organ in trio sonatas is a very strong indication that the work is intended for church when the title fails to make that clear.

As in earlier publications the titles specify the number of principal parts and make separate mention of the continuo. With two or three solo instruments a number of different combinations are possible, two of which proved particularly attractive. One consisted of two treble parts and basso continuo; the other, of two trebles, bass, and basso continuo. Not uncommon is a third kind, a duo sonata for treble and bass. Examples 1.1, 1.2, and 1.3 show characteristic samples of the three kinds.

In the *sonata a due* by Bononcini (1672), example 1.1, all the action is in the two violins. The subject is imitated by the second violin in bar 3, after which the two parts engage in motivic interplay. The basso continuo con-

Example 1.1.   G. M. Bononcini, *Sonata a due* for Two Violins and Basso Continuo, Opus 6, No. 4

Example 1.2.   G. Legrenzi, *Sonata a due* for Violin, Violone, and Basso Continuo, Opus 10, No. 4

tains no thematic material and the slowly-moving part simply furnishes the organist with the clues needed to provide an accompaniment.

In the *sonata a due* by Legrenzi (1682), example 1.2, the principal parts are played by violin and violone. The continuo is a simplified version of the bass, having much of the fast motion removed. The bass is an obbligato part and could not be left out without a significant loss of contrapuntal material. The same observations apply to the *sonata a tre* by Corelli (1681), the main difference being that the piece employs two violins instead of one (ex. 1.3).

These examples, which are representative of the Italian church sonata, clearly illustrate the relationship between the bass and the basso continuo. The bass, when included, takes a prominent part in imitations and imitative interplay. The continuo in such cases is a simplified version of the contrapuntal bass with all the florid motion left out. In works without a separate bass part the continuo looks much the same and contains little if any thematic or motivic material.

While the church sonata repertory as a whole conforms to this description, there are exceptions, all involving music in which an active bass part is either optional or given to the organ alone. In the duo sonatas of Bassani's *Sinfonie a due, e tre instromenti* (1683b) the cello has an animated concer-

Example 1.3.   A. Corelli, *Sonata a tre* for Two Violins, Violone or Archlute, and Basso
Continuo, Opus 1, No. 10

tante part that is optional. These sonatas have no imitations in the bass while those *a tre* do, and in those the cello is obligatory. In other words, the concertante bass part, though very prominent, is considered optional unless it contains imitations.

A similar situation is found in G. B. Mazzaferrata's *Sonate a due violini con un bassetto viola se piace* (1674). The bass is a concertante part, and even though it contains scattered instances of imitations these are less prominent than when the part is obligatory. Like Bassani, Mazzaferrata was active in Ferrara, and this may have something to do with the similarities between their works.

In some works where the bass is imitative the part is either optional or given to the organ. G. Colombi's opus 4 (1676) contains, according to the title, duo sonatas with an optional bass, but the pieces are in fact genuine trios. In the table of contents the two last sonatas are marked "for two violins," and for these there is no bass part. Here the composer seems to acknowledge the general meaning of the expression *a due*, yet in the rest of the collection he does not. A similar situation is found in B. Tonini's *sonate a tre* for two violins and organ with an optional cello (1697). In contrast to Colombi, Tonini acknowledges that the pieces are trios, yet the bass is optional. Still another twist on the same theme is found in P. Degli Antoni's *Suonate a violino solo* (1686). The bass is contrapuntal so that the pieces are in fact duos, yet the accompaniment is only for organ. Similar circumstances are found in works by Colombi (1673) and Albergati (1683).

The common factor in all these cases is the optional bass in pieces where it could be expected to be obligatory. The bass instrument could be left out even when it contained imitations. This alternative had obvious commercial appeal in allowing performance by two violins and continuo when a bass instrument was not available.

As far as bass-line doubling is concerned, these examples, if anything, argue against it. The bass part may be left out even when it is expected to be obligatory. In order to support the case for doubling there would have to be a bass part added in cases where it is not contrapuntally important. Such cases do indeed exist, but they represent a sideline of the church sonata tradition leading toward orchestral music.

Late Seventeenth-Century Interest in Orchestral Sonorities

During the second half of the seventeenth century the Italians took a noticeable interest in enriched instrumental sonorities. In Rome the string ensemble accompanying oratorios grew from two violins around 1660 to about ten or more in the 1670s (Liess 1957, 142–55). Initially used only in works of vocal nature, the large instrumental groups soon became a proving ground for the development of instrumental music. It is hardly coincidence that Corelli's concertos developed in Rome at just this time.

The interest in enriched instrumental sonorities was also clearly present in the musical establishment at another important center at the time: the basilica of San Petronio in Bologna. Especially significant are the developments that took place from the time when Maurizio Cazzati was hired as *maestro di cappella* (1657) until the orchestra, for financial reasons, was abandoned in 1695. Concerted vocal music was a prominent part of the San Petronio repertory, but, as in Rome, independent orchestral music also found fertile ground. A striking feature of all this music is the prominence given the bass; the performance material shows an unusual number of bass instruments participating (Enrico 1976, tables 1, 3; Schnoebelen 1969, 44). Moreover, several of the bass parts are identical to the basso continuo (Schnoebelen 1969, 47–48).

The best-known works performed at San Petronio were the trumpet concertos by Giuseppe Torelli (1658–1709), but the repertory also included pieces entitled *sinfonie*. In the seventeenth century this term was attached to a variety of different kinds of pieces, and in ways that defy categorization. At San Petronio, for example, the terms *sinfonia* and *concerto* were often used interchangeably (Berger 1951, 362–64). But whatever term is used, the pieces were intended for orchestral performance.

The title *sinfonie* shows up in publications by Bolognese composers around 1680 but these works are very different from those found at San Petronio. For example, the *sinfonie a tre* in Torelli's opus 5 (1692) are indistinguishable from church sonatas *a tre*. In the preface, however, Torelli explains that the work is intended for orchestral performance. In terms of the usage at San Petronio, this explanation would indicate why the work is entitled *sinfonie* rather than *sonate da chiesa*.

Torelli's opus 5 contains two bass parts, one of which duplicates the basso continuo. This feature, found in a few other publications at this time, has been taken as proof that baroque sonatas need the doubling of the continuo line, even if another bass part is included. The presence of two bass parts, however, is only what one would expect to find in Bolognese music for large ensemble at this time. The work illustrates how pieces which in reality are church sonatas were performed orchestrally under the name of *sinfonie* and with the continuo line reinforced by an extra bass instrument.

Torelli's opus 1 (1686) also contains an added bass part. The pieces are similar in nature to those in opus 5, but the title is different: the earlier collection is called *Sonate a tre*. However, the purpose of the added bass was surely the same in the two collections, namely, to add strength to the continuo line in pieces performed orchestrally.

The interest in orchestral sonorities at San Petronio can be traced back to Maurizio Cazzati, the *maestro di capella* from 1657 to 1671. Among his works are several examples of instrumental works with reinforced basso continuo. The most important examples are the sonatas opus 35 (1665) for two to five instruments, some of which include a trumpet. Torelli, in his opus 1, assigns the added part to a regular bass instrument, a theorbo or a violone; Cazzati calls for theorbo or *contrabasso*. The double bass is an orchestral instrument which, generally speaking, is inappropriate in music with one player to a part. Several of the larger pieces in Cazzati's opus 35 imply orchestral performance. The sonatas for four strings and trumpet are nothing less than incipient concertos, so that both the doubling of the string parts and the support of the double bass are appropriate.

Cazzati's opus 18 (1656) contains duo sonatas for two violins and continuo; in this work the composer also doubles the bass with theorbo or violone. The performance of these pieces, identical to that of the duo sonatas in opus 35, illustrates Cazzati's predilection for orchestral sonorities in a repertory that traditionally was performed by soloists and continued in such a manner after Cazzati's time.

Another work that may belong to the category of incipient concertos is Arresti's *Suonate a 2 & a tre. Con la parte del violoncello a beneplacito* (1665). The cello part is very active but only occasionally imitative; the pieces are thus in effect *sonate a due*. Some passages in the work are marked "solo," and at times the second violin and bass create tutti effects in contrast to the violin solo. The result would be considerably enhanced by doubling of the various parts and the inclusion of the bass-line instrument.

The works with added bass parts were published within about a thirty-year span. After Torelli's opus 5 (1692) such parts were no longer found in church sonatas; by that time the concerto grosso had developed to a point where it was no longer necessary to adapt existing genres to the requirements of orchestral performance. The added bass parts fall outside of the main tradition of the church sonata, and there are no indications that this genre required reinforcement of the continuo part, except for the handful of compositions by composers associated with San Petronio who aimed at orchestral performance of their works.

4

Bass-Line Doubling
in Opera and Oratorio

Opera

The study of bass-line doubling in dramatic music poses fundamentally different questions from those encountered in the church sonata. Operas and oratorios were rarely published and the extant manuscript scores contain few if any performance indications. A few surviving playing parts, occasional payment records, and a few descriptions of performances is all the research material presently available. Nevertheless, opera and oratorio together provide a scantily documented but consistent picture of a practice of bass-line doubling with roots in the late sixteenth century.

Many of the early operas, Monteverdi's *Orfeo* among them, were written for celebrations in noble families such as weddings, anniversaries and birthdays. The musical part of such celebrations, known as "intermedii" or "intermezzi," have a long history in the sixteenth century. One such work stands in a pivotal position between old and new: the Florentine *Intermedii* performed at the Medici court in 1589 (Walker 1963; Brown 1973). The performance took place in a city where only a few years later opera was born. The principal composers of the yet-to-come music drama were all there: Cavalieri took charge of the musical arrangements; Peri and Caccini participated as performers.

The music of the Florentine *Intermedii* is all notated as polyphony with from three to thirty parts. A variety of combinations of voices is prescribed, from Peri's performance of the four-part *Dunque fra torbid'onde* as a solo accompanied only by a chitarrone, to massive conglomerations of several vocal choirs supported by lutes, trombones, viols, cornetti, etc. In some cases the instruments evidently doubled the vocal lines, as when a consort of strings participated with an equal number of voices in a four-part madrigal. At other times, the number, as well as the kinds of instruments chosen, suggests a different function. Of particular interest are the following instances:

> *Chi dal destino.* Madrigal, sung by six voices, accompanied by *leuto grosso, chitarrone,* and *basso di viola.*
>
> *O valorose Dio.* Performed by four voices, with harp and lira.
>
> *Io che l'onde raffreno.* Five-part madrigal, performed by one solo voice with lute, *chitarrone* and *archiviolata lira.*

In each case the accompaniment consists of one or more chordal instruments and one bowed instrument. The chordal instruments may have realized the bass or perhaps played from a score. The function of the other instruments is less clear. The lira used in *O valorose Dio* is a treble instrument so that it would not have been able to reinforce the bass, like the bass viol in *Chi dal destino.* Common to the three pieces is the combination of plucked instruments with sustaining instruments to form a small ensemble used for accompaniment.

The earliest dramatic works in the monodic style give few specifics on the instrumentation. Peri's *Euridice* (1600) employed four instruments: harpsichord, theorbo, lira, and a large lute; but nothing is known about how the instruments were combined. The preface to Cavalieri's *Rappresentatione di Anima e di Corpo* (1600), written by the librettist Guidotti, is more explicit. Two combinations of instruments were thought to be particularly suitable for the accompaniment: *lira doppia* (= lira da gamba), harpsichord, and chitarrone, or an *organo suave* with a chitarrone.

While the specific combinations of instruments vary considerably, they illustrate a predilection for certain combinations of sounds. Each of the accompanying groups mentioned above includes a sustaining instrument and one or more plucked ones. The sustaining instrument, when not an organ, is usually in the bass range. The combination most frequently encountered seems to be a plucked instrument in conjunction with a sustaining bass instrument.

Monteverdi's *Orfeo* (1609), first performed in 1607, contains the most explicit information about the use of continuo instruments of any baroque opera. The printed score contains detailed markings showing the instrumentation at the first performance. The combinations of continuo instruments is very much like those already encountered, with one exception: in the underworld scene in act 3 the reed organ is used alone and so is the *organo di legno.* In acts 2 and 4, however, the *organo di legno* is coupled with the chitarrone (Monteverdi 1609, 36, 39, 86).

The harpsichord was most often paired with the chitarrone and these two instruments were occasionally joined by a cello (Monteverdi 1609,

27–32, 36, 80). The combination of two plucked instruments, harpsichord and chitarrone, is somewhat peculiar in that both are capable of realizing the bass. The chitarrone, having a softer sound, would not add much volume to the harpsichord, and simultaneous realizations by both instruments create intonation problems. The fixed-pitch chords of the harpsichord often clash with those produced on the fretted chitarrone. A strong case can be made that the extended lutes, chitarrone and archlute, at times functioned as bass-line instruments and not for the realization of the bass (see chap. 13). This usage is particularly common in the church sonata where the contrapuntal bass part optionally may be performed by theorbo or violone. Using the chitarrone in a similar manner in *Orfeo* not only would ameliorate the intonation problems but also allow the plucked instrument to make extensive use of its strongest suit: the open strings in the lower register. The function of the chitarrone would in that case be somewhat similar to that of a double bass.

The variety of continuo instruments used in *Orfeo* represents a transitional stage in the development of opera. The organ was soon omitted, and Doni (ca. 1635, 1: 107) probably reflects a commonly held view when, in a discussion of opera from around 1635, he says that this instrument is best left for use in the churches. The harpsichord became the principal chordal instrument in opera, often joined by a theorbo, a bowed bass instrument, or both.

The first indication of a more standardized continuo occurs in Monteverdi's *Il combattimento di Tancredi e Clorinda,* published in 1638 in the eighth book of madrigals, but first performed in 1624. The preface describes the instruments employed at the first performance as a consort made up of members of the violin family, and one *contrabasso da gamba* to go with the harpsichord. These two instruments apparently play continuously throughout the work, including the recitatives. In light of later operatic practices it seems likely that the contrabasso played the bass in its proper register rather than an octave below.

The orchestra in seventeenth-century Venetian opera houses included two harpsichords, two theorbos, cello, and violone (Selfridge-Field 1975, 39), but nothing is known about their use in the continuo accompaniment. A serenata by A. Cesti performed in Florence in 1664 contains unusually complete information on the continuo instrumentation (Wellesz 1913–14, 124):

> The voices, when singing alone, in duets and in trios were accompanied by a large harpsichord with two registers, the theorbo, and the *contrabasso*; the eight-part choruses had, in addition to the mentioned instruments, a *basso di viola*, and [the] little spinet and sometimes the whole orchestra.

[Le voci a solo, a 2. e 3. furono Accompagnate da una Spinetta grossa a 2 registri; dalla Tiorba e dal Contrabasso, e li Cori a otto oltre li detti Strumenti, da un basso di Viola e dalla Spinettina, et alle Tutti Insieme.]

The implication seems to be that the harpsichord, theorbo, and contrabasso played all the time, presumably also in the recitatives. This impression is strengthened by the records from the court of Cardinal Ottoboni in Rome covering the period 1689–1740. For the performance of operas, several full scores were prepared for the harpsichord and lute. Hansell (1966, 400) noticed a shortage of bass parts and concluded that some of the *violoni* also must have played from scores.

Benedetto Marcello, for all his facetiousness, makes telling observations about the use of the cello in opera. In *Il teatro alla moda* (ca. 1723, 49) he describes the liberties taken by the cello virtuoso in accompanying the recitatives an octave higher, leaving out passages at will in the arias, and introducing different variations every evening. Marcello's comments are all directed toward excesses in the manner of playing; he evidently took the participation of the cellist for granted in arias as well as recitatives.

Oratorio

In oratorio, as in opera, documentation for the use of bowed instruments is scanty. Less is known about the early part of the century than is the case in opera. However, more playing parts are preserved, and certain oratorio scores contain more information than is normally found in opera scores.

The performing parts for a large number of late seventeenth-century oratorios are preserved at the library of the Oratorio dei Filippini in Naples. The material is in many cases incomplete, but where parts for bass-line instruments are extant, they support the findings in opera. Representative of this repertory is the oratorio *La morte di Maria Magdalena* (I-Nf, MS 425) by Tomasso Pagano (d. ca. 1690), a prolific composer of such works. The instrumental bass part is unmarked and may have been intended for a bowed instrument, an archlute, or both. It contains all the music from beginning to end. In the recitatives the vocal line is included, but only the first words of the text. This format is standard in all the oratorios by Pagano (I-Nf, MS 425, MS 426) as well as his contemporaries represented in the same collection.

A few works contain more detailed markings, such as the *Oratorio a 3 voci* by D. Fregiotti, another seventeenth-century composer (I-Nf, MS 436). The instruments required are two organs, two cellos, and one or possibly two archlutes. The principal archlute apparently played from the same part as the first cello, because in the obbligato arias the two instruments are notated on separate staves. The participation of another archlute, playing from the other cello part, seems likely; that part has no divisi sections so there would be no reason to mention the second instrument. As in Pagano's oratorios the vocal line is given in the recitatives.

Oratorios from Bologna show a preference for the theorbo as bass-line instrument. That is the case in the anonymous *La sepulture di Christo* (I-Bsp, MS P.54.1), possibly by the cellist Petronio Franceschini and reflecting the musical style of around 1670. The identical parts for harpsichord and theorbo include the vocal line in the recitatives, but otherwise only the bass. The cello, which does not participate in the recitatives, plays in the arias even when the other string instruments are excluded.

The San Petronio archive contains what appears to be complete sets of performing parts for two oratorios by G. Perti, dating from the last two decades of the seventeenth century (I-Bsp, MS P.55.3; MS P.57.1). The scores presumably served the keyboard, which is not identified, but in other Bolognese oratorios is a harpsichord. The archlute participates continuously, also in the recitatives. The cello, on the other hand, plays only in the orchestral tutti sections.

Pirro Albergati's *Cantate e oratorii spirituali*, published in 1714, contains two oratorios and a number of sacred cantatas. The harpsichord continuo is reinforced by an identical part for theorbo or violone.

Summary

While many aspects of continuo performance in dramatic music remain obscure, the question of reinforcing the bass part can be answered with some certainty. The harpsichord is always joined by another instrument: an extended lute, a bowed bass instrument, or both. The supporting instrument plays the bass line only, even when it is of the lute family. The bass-line instrument plays continually throughout the work, in recitatives as well as in arias.

The contrabasso is occasionally mentioned as the supporting instrument and that adds credibility to the argument that the extended lutes also played the bass part in the lower octave, on the open strings. However, with the rise of the basso obbligato aria, which requires an agile instrument in the normal bass range, the double bass is unlikely to have been used in arias after about 1670.

5

Secular Vocal Music

Monody and Cantata to 1670

The performance conventions in the early seventeenth-century monodic repertory seem strangely inconsistent. When occuring in a dramatic work the monody was accompanied by at least two instruments, while a similar piece performed in a drawing room required only a chordal instrument. Since the musical style is the same, the difference in performance is very likely a result of acoustical considerations. Operas and oratorios were performed in relatively large halls where the harpsichord tone carried poorly and needed to be reinforced. Significantly, the organs in Monteverdi's *Orfeo* at times play alone, their sustained sound having enough body to carry without reinforcement. The use of bass instruments together with the harpsichord was not intended to strengthen the bass per se; if so, the bass of the organ continuo should have been strengthened as well. Thus, when monodies were performed in an intimate setting, a chordal instrument alone provided all the needed support.

Monteverdi's eighth book of madrigals (1638) provides an instructive case of the difference in performance between dramatic works and vocal ensemble music. In the dramatic ballet *Il combattimento di Tancredi e Clorinda* a preface explains that a contrabasso played along with the harpsichord all the time (Monteverdi 1926–42, 8:132). The specific mention of this instrument indicates that its use was exceptional within the context of the publication. When Monteverdi wants a contrabasso in a madrigal, he invariably notates it on a separate staff. Such parts are not continuous and serve an entirely different function from the doubling in *Il combattimento*. In *Vago augeletto* (Monteverdi 1926–42, 8:222), for seven voices, two violins, basso continuo and contrabasso, the latter is used only for tutti effects, i.e., when all voices and instruments participate. The sections for one or a few voices are consistently accompanied by the basso continuo alone. The same is true of *Altri canti d'amor* (Monteverdi 1926–42, 8:2). In other words, secular vocal music, even when requiring a fairly large ensemble, does not require any strengthening of the basso continuo line as does dramatic music.

With the growth of the solo cantata around 1640, a repertory different from the earlier monody comes into existence and the possibility exists that other performance conventions were introduced. Several accounts of performances by prominent singers at this time suggest that the accompaniment still was carried out by a single chordal instrument. The French gamba player Maugars visited Rome in 1639 and says about the celebrated Leonora Baroni that "she does not need to ask the help of a theorbo player or a violinist, without one of which her singing would be imperfect, for she herself plays these instruments perfectly." (MacClintock 1979, 122–23)

Pietro della Valle also comments that Leonora accompanied herself on the archlute (ca. 1640, 2:256).

Doni's description of the singing of Adriana Baroni, Leonora's mother, not only documents the use of a single instrument for the accompaniment but also implies that more instruments participated in stage performances. Doni (ca. 1635, 111) prefers the simpler accompaniment and uses the occasion to attack operatic practice:

> Whoever has heard Adriana sing while playing her own harp will know what kind of accompaniment is required in music with expression and pathos. And whoever says that such simplicity is not suitable for the stage, for my part, I think he has a corrupted taste.

> [Che ha sentito cantare Adriana al suono della sua medesima Arpa, avra potuto conoscere qual sorte di accompagnamenti richiede una Musica efficace, e patetica. E chi giudichera che questa semplicita non convenga alla scena, quanto a me io credo, che abbia il gusto corrotto.]

These descriptions relate to performances in Rome in the period when Luigi Rossi and G. Carissimi were making inroads with their solo cantatas. The most celebrated singers still performed according to Caccini's recommendation, accompanying themselves on a plucked instrument.

The accompaniment of vocal solos by a chordal instrument alone thus continued into the period of the solo cantata. Toward the end of the century the situation changed as the style of the arias changed. This development, which started with the opera aria, had noticeable effects on the performance of cantatas, creating a rationale for the addition of a cello to perform the bass part.

The Basso Obbligato Aria

In the 1670s the aria in operas and oratorios underwent a drastic change. The bass of the continuo aria, which up to this time had been completely subordinate to the voice, now took on the character of an obbligato part. Marcello (ca.1723, 22) described this kind of piece as an aria with *basso solo obbligato*; a somewhat simpler expression, *basso obbligato aria*, will be used below.

The new kind of aria represented nothing less than a minor stylistic revolution and had far-reaching consequences. Once the idea of an obbligato part in the bass was accepted, the way was paved to introduce such parts in the treble as well. The treble obbligato has received more attention, but there can be little doubt that its origin is in the basso obbligato aria.

The sudden prominence of the bass did not spring from a single source, but from a series of related developments. These are best described in terms of their background — the aria style common around the middle of the seventeenth century.

An opera from around 1660 normally contains 50–60 arias. The melodic material is concentrated in the vocal part. The instrumental parts are of little if any intrinsic musical interest and serve primarily as a backdrop for the voice. This is particularly true of the arias with basso continuo accompaniment, which make up about four-fifths of the total. Not only is the continuo subordinate to the voice, but there is almost a complete lack of ritornelli.

The orchestra participates in about one-fifth of the arias. One or two may have continuous string accompaniment, consisting of sustained chords. These provide a neutral blanket of sound, supporting the voice without attracting attention. In other arias the orchestra plays ritornelli that are separated from the vocal sections without overlap. Ritornelli occur at the beginning and end, and short orchestral passages may appear in the middle of an aria as well. The opening ritornello regularly features the subsequent phrase of the voice, and a similar relationship often exists with internal ritornelli.

Around 1670 the bass line in the aria changed from a subordinate role to sharing in the presentation of melodic material. The change showed up in three different ways. In one of these the bass is active whenever the voice rests. The opening phrase is first presented in the bass and repeated by the voice. Subsequently the bass part may include brief passages at phrase endings, which at times are extended into lengthy ritornellos. During the vocal sections, however, the bass is distinctly subordinate. The layout is strikingly similar to that of the older aria with instruments, the difference being that the bass provides the ritornellos instead of the orchestra. The bass-line instrument, most likely a cello, now takes on a soloistic function it had not had before.

The second type of aria is similar to the first in that the voice and the bass share in the same material and that the opening phrase is first pre-

Example 1.4.   A. Stradella, Aria from *San Giovanni Battista*

sented instrumentally. But here the bass is active throughout the piece, engaging in imitations and motivic interplay with the voice. This kind of piece is in many respects similar to a chamber duet in featuring two parts of equal musical importance. Example 1.4 shows an aria of this kind from Stradella's oratorio *San Giovanni Battista* (I-Bc, MS BB/361, fol. 18v). The soloistic nature of the bass is reflected in the part being earmarked for the first cello. Such indications are very rare, but needed in this case because this kind of aria with its soloistic use of the cello was a novelty.

In the third kind of aria the bass gains prominence from the free use of ostinatos. Two kinds of ostinato occur, one traditional, the other progressive. The traditional type, well-known from earlier monodies, features an inconspicuous bass pattern in the middle to lower bass range and contains little if any rhythmic variation. Not intended to draw attention to itself because of its melodic qualities, the ostinato serves as a structural framework for the piece.

The progressive ostinato aria contains fast figuration which often

Example 1.5.   Ostinato patterns from A. Stradella's *San Giovanni Battista*

a.   "Anco il cielo"

b.   "Anco il sol"

moves into the tenor range. The voice and bass are given separate identities through phrases and motives of a contrasting nature. The ostinato is first stated alone and then repeated as the accompaniment for the first vocal phrase. It may be restated several times, alternating with motivically related passages, but sometimes the only complete statements are those at the beginning. Keeping the ostinato going was of less concern than giving the bass a character different from that of the vocal part.

Both kinds of ostinato aria are found in Stradella's oratorio *San Giovanni Battista*, and their performance differed significantly. The traditional ostinato aria, such as "Anco il cielo" (I-Bc, MS BB/361, fol. 22v), employs all the basses of the orchestra (ex. 1.5a). The progressive ostinato aria "Anco il sol" (I-Bc, MS BB/361, fol. 76v), on the other hand, calls for the first cello only, and the soloistic nature of the part fully justifies such treatment (ex. 1.5b). In the progressive ostinato aria the bass is not an accompaniment but a complement to the voice. Containing significant melodic material and elaborate passage work, the bass part needs to be thought of as a true obbligato part and performed accordingly on the cello.

The various kinds of basso obbligato arias soon showed up in the solo cantata and came to dominate the genre. Many arias of this type were written by such prominent composers as Stradella, A. Scarlatti, and Handel, to mention just a few. The harpsichord alone cannot do full justice to the obbligato part since the realization inevitably obscures the bass line. This circumstance provides the musical rationale for including a bass-line instrument in the performance of solo cantatas.

Solo cantatas, whether published or in manuscript, are always notated in score. Separate parts for a cello are very rare and if this instrument were to participate in the performance the player would have had to read from the same part as the continuo player. It is perhaps no coincidence that indications of such a practice first appear around 1670. C. Grossi's *L'An-fione musiche da camera, o per tavola* (1675) contains a part intended for the cello and the basso continuo together. While not proving that the cello always was used in solo cantatas, this publication shows that such usage was possible at the time when the basso obbligato aria came into existence. The strongest evidence that the cello was used in the solo cantata is distinctly second-hand and from a much later time. Burney (1776–89, 4:169), apparently relying primarily on the account of Geminiani, says about the performance of Scarlatti's cantatas,

> The violoncello parts of many of these cantatas were so excellent that whoever was able to do them justice was thought a supernatural being. Geminiani used to relate that Franceschelli, a celebrated performer on the violoncello at the beginning of this century, accompanied one of these cantatas at Rome so admirably, while Scarlatti was at the harpsichord, that the company being good Catholics and living in a country where miraculous powers have not yet ceased, were firmly persuaded it was not Franceschelli who had played the violoncello, but an angel that had descended and assumed his shape.

Burney takes the participation of the cello in Scarlatti's cantatas for granted. Since the scores invariably contain parts for only voice and continuo, the cellist probably read from the same part as the keyboard player.

The Bolognese cellist Giuseppe Jacchini (16[?]-1727) was especially known for his accompaniment of singers (Vatielli 1927, 140–41). Though the cello at times may have been used alone for the accompaniment, it would seem that Jacchini's fame must have come from the more common situation when the cello was used in conjunction with the harpsichord.

Francesco Gasparini, in his cantatas published in 1695, seems to imply that the participation of a bass-line instrument is taken for granted:

> To the music lovers: In some of the arias you will find two bass parts, one of which is for the ease of accompanying. It has to some extent been necessary to make adjustments for the sake of printing, and I have not been able totally to show my intentions. Where, however, there is a soprano or violin clef above the bass, that is played with the right hand, as if it were tablature. It will also suffice to use archlute and cello.

> [A gl'Amatori Della Musica: Trovarete in alcune Arie dui bassi uno per commodo, o facilita di accompagnare; essendo stato necessario anche accomodarse alla Stampa, che non ho potuto totalmente dimostrar la mia intenzione. Pero dove si trovano sopra il basso alcune chiavi di Canto, o Violino si soneranno con la mano destra in forma d'intavolatura. Ivi potranno ancora sodisfarsi l'Arcileuto, e Violoncello.]

The alternate continuo instrumentation mentioned at the end includes two instruments, one for the realization, and another for the bass line. Two instruments would presumably also be needed when the chordal instrument is the harpsichord.

Three of Gasparini's arias have two bass parts, one of them a simplified version of the other "for the ease of accompanying" on the harpsichord (Gasparini 1695, 38, 76, 113). The last one, *Il mio pianto* (ex. 4.11), illustrates the division of labor between the two instruments. One part contains animated figuration evidently intended for the cello. The other contains mostly the harmonically active notes needed for the continuo realization.

The inclusion of two bass parts is unusual and most often unnecessary. Continuo manuals recommend that the fast figuration be left to the bass-line instrument and that the chordal instrument play a simplified line of the kind written out by Gasparini. His reason for including two parts is that in some cases the continuo bass contains progressions that would not have been immediately clear if the player of the chordal instrument had used the florid part.

One instrumental work may have a bearing on the use of cello in cantata arias: G. Taglietti's *Pensieri musicali* (1707). Written for solo violin with cello and continuo accompaniment, the pieces in this collection are unusual in adopting the form of the da capo aria. The cello occasionally has melodic passages, but most of the time it is strictly accompanimental, doubling the continuo line. Thus there is no contrapuntal reason to include the bass-line instrument. Taglietti's *Pensieri* probably reflects a preference for having a sustaining instrument play the bass, in other words, of doubling the basso continuo.

While the use of a bass-line instrument in solo cantatas must have occurred with some frequency, it was hardly an established practice. Gasparini's implication (1695) that the cello should be used in the cantatas of his opus 1 is within a few years contradicted in a similar publication, Bernardo Gaffi's *Cantate da camera a voce sola* (1700). Not only are the two collections brought out by the same publisher, Mascardi in Rome, but Gaffi's preface is very similar to Gasparini's, down to the choice of words:

> To music lovers, from the composer. If one finds arias with two bass parts and the upper one with violin or tenor clef, one can use a violin or a *violone*. Lacking these, the ingenuity of a good harpsichord player may supply both, so the parts in violin clef are taken with the right hand, and the others with the left, the composer not intending to present cantatas with instruments, but only, for your greater edification and delight, to have the harpsichord play as if from tablature.

> [L'autore a gl'amatori della Musica. Si troveranno alcune Arie con due Bassi, e quello di sopra con mutationi di chiavi di Violino o Tenore, ivi potranno sodisfarsi il Violino o Violone & alla mancanza di questi potra supplire la virtu di un buon Sonatore di Cembalo con fare l'uno & altro Basso, cioè la Chiave di Violino con la mano destra, e le altre con la sinistra, non havendo l'Autore intentione di presentarvi Cantate con Istromenti, ma solo di far suonare il Cembalo a uso d'Intavolatura, per vostro maggior studio e diletto.]

Gaffi suggests that the added parts may be played by a violin or a violone, but nowhere does he imply that either of these instruments should participate all the time. On the contrary, the composer specifically says that he is not writing "cantatas with instruments" and there is no reason to believe that a bass-line instrument would have been needed except where specified.

Some of the cantatas that Handel wrote in Italy appear to have been performed without a bass-line instrument. During the period 1707–10 he was occasionally employed by the Ruspoli family, and part of his duty was to write cantatas for their Sunday afternoon gatherings. The payment records show that cello and violone were added to the permanent ensemble in 1708 (Kirkendale 1967, 228ff., 271–72). Since no bass players were hired separately, the 21 cantatas performed in 1707 made use of only harpsichord. One of the cantatas from 1708, *Mentre il tutto e in furore*, contains an aria in which the bass features an ostinato pattern with fast repeated notes (Handel 1858–94, 50:147). This kind of figuration is very awkward to play on the keyboard, but is idiomatic to a bowed instrument. No similar figuration is used in the cantatas from 1707 and it is possible that Handel wrote the part with the newly appointed cellist in mind, thus taking advantage of his presence.

Summary

Secular song in Italy was until about 1670 accompanied by a chordal instrument alone. The basso obbligato aria, which appeared at this time, provided a musical rationale for including a bass-line instrument in addition to the chordal instrument. Both players would have read from the same part and that was plausible at the time the basso obbligato aria was created. While there can be little doubt that a bass-line instrument often was included in the performance of cantatas, it is uncertain to what extent this usage became a general practice.

6

Sacred Vocal Music

Introduction

The employment of bass-line instruments in sacred vocal music in certain respects parallels that in the solo cantata. At the beginning of the baroque period bass instruments were not used in conjunction with the continuo. They start to appear after the middle of the seventeenth century and gain increasing currency in the eighteenth. In the solo cantata this practice is based on a musical rationale: the melodic and contrapuntal qualities of the bass demand a separate instrument even though separate performing parts are not found. Sacred vocal music, in contrast, shows no clear rationale for the inclusion of bass-line instruments even though performing parts are found with increasing frequency after 1720.

Sacred vocal music encompasses a large and varied repertory for solo voice, small vocal ensembles, choir, multiple choirs, or a combination of two or more of these possibilities. An instrumental group may also be added. At its most elaborate, the combination of these forces in concerted works resulted in some of the most impressive and least known music of the baroque era.

With so many different genres of sacred music it would not be surprising to find some variety in the use of bass instruments. Moreover, local traditions may differ and also change in the course of time. These variations in the use of bass instruments can be illustrated by comparing practices in Rome to those in Bergamo, and by looking at the concerted music used for important celebrations.

Rome and Bergamo: Different Performing Traditions?

If circumstances in Rome are representative of a general practice, it appears that throughout the baroque period the bulk of Italian sacred music was performed without any other accompaniment than the organ. The absence of bass-line instruments reinforcing the basso continuo in the early part of the seventeenth century is consistently reaffirmed in later sources pertinent to Roman practices. The descriptions by A. Maugars on his visit to Rome in 1639 are particularly interesting in specifying the instruments he heard in the churches. On one occasion ten choirs were employed, each one accompanied by a portative organ. In performances of motets Maugars heard "one, two, or three violins with the organ, and with archlutes playing certain dance tunes and answering each other" (MacClintock 1979, 118).

The absence of any mention of bass instruments is striking, the more so since Maugars, himself a gambist, is likely to have taken a special interest in such instruments. If bass instruments were present it would seem like a given that Maugars would have commented upon their use, especially since elsewhere he goes on at some length about the state of gamba playing in Rome in less than complimentary language (MacClintock 1979, 121).

The performance material, both manuscripts and publications, points to basso continuo performance by the organ alone. In the motets by Orazio Benevoli (1605–72), *maestro di cappella* at the Vatican from 1645 until his death, the continuo part always duplicates the lowest voice part. There are no parts for other instruments than the organ, nor any other indications that the continuo should be reinforced (Bryden 1951, 102, 120). The same is true of the motets of Giacomo Carissimi (1604–74). The organ alone plays the continuo part and bass instruments are not used except as part of the instrumental group that sometimes is included (Jones 1982, 1:234, 237–38).

The absence of bass-line instruments for the regular services in Roman churches in the eighteenth century suggests that the continuo accompaniment remained the same as at the time of Benevoli and Carissimi. Giuseppe Ottavio Pitoni (1657–1743) was active in Rome from 1686, from 1719 at the Cappella Giulia at the Vatican, succeeding Domenico Scarlatti. The payment records of the three main churches where he worked, covering the period from 1694 until his death, show that nowhere did the permanent musical ensemble consist of anything more than singers and organists (Gmeinwieser 1973, 70–73).

The absence of bass players in the churches is matched by the absence of performing parts for their instruments. The large amount of music in manuscript left by Chiti shows no indication of the use of bass-line instruments except in works where they are part of an orchestra (Gmeinwieser 1968, vol. 2).

Practices in Bergamo differed considerably from those in Rome. According to the payment records at S. Maria Maggiore, bass-line instruments were extensively used from some time in the late seventeenth century. The amount of the payments suggests that the duties of the bass players were similar to those of the organist. Records show the presence of bass players over a long period of time and suggest that their duties may have been of the same magnitude as those of the organist. The records were examined by R. Bowman, who chose to focus on certain specific years between 1650 and 1720. In 1687 the violone player asked for a raise because he had to accompany the organist all the time; his salary in 1671 was about half of the organist's (Bowman 1981, 351). The request must have met with success because in 1695 the two have salaries that are very close: L. 553 for the organist and L. 504 for the violone player. The first violinist, in contrast, earned considerably less: L. 385 (Bowman 1981, 333). In 1699 the double bass player was accorded salary and status comparable to that of the cello and first violin players (Bowman 1981, 351).

All this suggests that the bass players had important duties, perhaps exceeding those of the first violinist. Particularly revealing is an entry from 1720 when all instrumentalists were excused from the service except the double bass player whose presence apparently was indispensable (Bowman 1981, 351). And though the specific duties of the bass players are not known, it is quite likely that they played with the organ in all the music that was performed.

Seventeenth-century publications of sacred music overwhelmingly support the Roman practices because bass parts duplicating the basso continuo are rare indeed. This picture changes, however, in the early eighteenth century. By 1720, the time the double bass player in Bergamo is refused leave, the use of bass-line instruments in sacred music is distinctly on the increase. This development has its roots in the concerted church music and seems to have started around 1660.

Concerted Music

The most elaborate church music of the seventeenth century is surely the concerted works. Early in the century these might involve a variety of combinations of voices and instruments, but eventually a more standardized ensemble evolved. It consists of solo singers, ripieno singers, and an instrumental group with two violins and sometimes a bass instrument, all, of course, accompanied by the organ continuo. This combination is found in L. Gallerano's *Messa e salmi concertati*, first published in Venice in 1629 and reissued in 1641. The twelve parts are arranged into three choirs and the preface explains how the pieces in the collection are performed. It turns out that the third choir is optional and always serves as ripieno. The second choir is instrumental, consisting of two violins and chitarrone, and that is the group of interest for the present purpose.

The instrumental group sometimes consists of only two violins and no bass instrument, as in G. Rovetta's *Messa e salmi* (1639). When bass instruments are included there is often a choice. Paolo Cornetti's *Motetti concertati* (1638) mentions three instruments: chitarrone, bassoon, or violone.

When the cello is included it does not double the continuo line. In Cavalli's *Musiche sacre* (1656) the instrumental group consists of two violins and "violoncino," i.e., cello. This instrument is part of the orchestra and plays only together with the violins, resting when they rest. In the preface Cavalli understandably asks that the the string instruments be seated together; if the cello had been part of the continuo it would have made more sense to have it situated close to the organist. The preface also makes clear that the cello part is optional. The printer, in a separate note, seconds that statement and adds that the part may be performed by chitarrone or bassoon, or another similar instrument. Both recommendations reflect usage commonly encountered in publications from the middle of the seventeenth century.

Large-scale concerted works without a part for bass-line instrument continue to be published until late in the seventeenth century. Increasingly, however, such works include an extra bass part duplicating the organ continuo, to be played by the violone or the theorbo. Another bass part for the orchestra, like the one in Cavalli's *Musiche sacre*, may be included as well.

The earliest examples of identical parts for organ and bass-line instruments occur in works by Mauritio Cazzati shortly after he had become *maestro di cappella* at San Petronio in Bologna in 1657. Three sets of masses (1660b, 1663, 1666) all feature solo and ripieno voices and an instrumental group consisting of two violins. The continuo line is shared by the organ and "violone or theorbo."

Cazzati remains the only composer to add extra bass parts in his publications until after 1680. Thereafter such parts appear with increasing frequency and soon become standard in concerted vocal music. The lead is taken by Bolognese composers such as Albergati (1687), Colonna (1691) and Bassani (1690), who kept close ties with Bologna though employed in neighboring Ferrara and Modena. In many of these works the orchestra is expanded to include violas, sometimes tenor violas, and, at a later time, wind instruments.

The presence of extra bass parts in vocal concerted music coincides closely with the emergence of such parts in church sonatas and *sinfonie*, works intended for orchestral performance. Whether in vocal or instrumental music, the need for bass instruments is associated with the use of large ensembles. In both kinds of repertories the doubling of the basso continuo line is associated with composers connected to San Petronio in Bologna.

The continuous parts for bass instruments are found not only in publications, but also in the extensive manuscript collection at San Petronio (Schnoebelen 1969, 47–48). But the published bass parts are important in showing that when bass instruments are needed the printers were willing to incur the extra expense of providing separate parts. That stands to reason, because for a seated cellist to read over the shoulder of the organist would in many churches be a difficult if not impossible task. In church music, therefore, a practice of doubling the basso continuo line would need to be documented by the existence of appropriate parts for the bass line instrument.

Bass-Line Instruments in Other than Concerted Music

Bass-line instruments eventually found their way into repertories other than the large-scale concerted works, though more slowly. In music for double chorus Bassani provides the earliest example with his Psalms, opus 30, published in Bologna in 1704. Each choir is accompanied by an organ and either "theorbo or violone." Two decades later such parts show up in works for a single choir as well as double chorus in works by Bellinzani (1718), Albergati (1721) and Silvani (1720, 1724).

Even in Rome, where the permanent musical ensemble in churches did not include bass-line instruments, extra players would be hired for festive occasions. During Pitoni's tenure at the Vatican, 1719–43, a number of cellos and double basses were hired for polychoral performances as the only extra instrumentalists. The number of bass instruments corresponded roughly to the number of organs used, so it appears that each chordal instrument was paired with either a cello or a double bass. Pitoni had no instrumentalists available other than organists so that most performances were accompanied by the organ alone (Gmeinwieser 1973, 73–76).

In music for solo voices the organ is more frequently joined by a bass-line instrument than in choral music. The reason is probably that sacred arias, like those in secular solo cantatas, acquire musically significant bass lines at the end of the seventeenth century so that the added instrument is needed.

Bassani, as early as 1683, published a collection for three solo voices with organ and "violone or theorbo." Similar collections appeared in the next 30 years with some frequency by composers such as by Bassani (1693a, 1701) and Albergati (1691, 1702, 1715). Equally important, such works showed up in manuscript collections, though not in great numbers, and not with any consistency.

The inconsistency in the use of bass-line instruments in sacred music is reflected in the recommendations of Zaccharia Tevo (1705, 360–62). In large-scale concerted works with instruments, the violone and the theorbo play the basso continuo while a number of other instruments are mentioned as appropriate for the orchestral bass part. In other kinds of sacred music the composer is free to choose whether or not to use instruments. Works for solo voice may employ two violins, or two violins and bass, or all the instruments used in concerted works with the violone and the theorbo doubling the basso continuo (Tevo 1705, 362).

Tevo's remarks confirm the validity of taking the presence of playing parts as a reliable guide to the use of bass-line instruments in sacred music. Thus, in a well cataloged collection a survey of the contents should tell how the practice of bass-line instruments developed later on. Fortunately, such a catalog exists for the large collection of sacred music covering the period 1600 to 1800, at the Basilica of Saint Francis in Assisi (Sartori 1962).

The music from the seventeenth century in the Assisi collection never contains bass parts doubling the continuo line. In the early eighteenth century such doubling occurs, though not with any consistency. Of the seven works for solo voice by Pietro Benedetti (1685–1730), for example, five employ the organ alone while two have an added part for cello. A similar situation is found in the works of Francesco Maria Benedetti (1688–1746), though all his works that employ violins also have a cello part.

Further into the eighteenth century, bass parts are increasingly included with the organ. The eleven works of Padre Martini all contain the extra bass part, and several contain parts for both cello and violone or double bass. Toward the end of the century works with only organ become the exception rather than the rule. Agostino Ricci, whose dated works fall between 1772 and 1786, left all together twenty-seven works with performing parts for voices and organ. Twenty-two contain additional parts for cello and violone or double bass, and one has a cello part, while four have no instrumental parts other than for organ. A similar situation is found in the works of all other composers from this period who are represented in the Assisi collection.

Summary

The use of bass-line instruments to reinforce the basso continuo line in sacred music went through a number of different stages during the seventeenth and eighteenth centuries. Doubling of the basso continuo was unheard of until about 1660. At that time scattered cases appeared in large-scale concerted works involving an instrumental group and solo and ripieno voices. From about 1680 bass-line doubling occurred in solo repertory as well as in choral music, but as exceptions rather than as the rule. Not until sometime after 1750 were cello and double bass included with the organ as a matter of course. In short, a general practice of bass-line doubling in sacred music did not develop during the baroque period but came into existence sometime in the late eighteenth century.

7

Bass and Basso Continuo in Secular Instrumental Music: Either, Or, or Both?

The Early Seventeenth Century

The mature chamber sonata represents the full development of secular instrumental music for small ensembles in the baroque era. The genre emerges around 1670 and is fully developed by 1700. The chamber sonata has its roots in dance music, and further back, in the three-part vocal music of the Renaissance. Through the entire time, the three-part texture is harmonically complete and in no need of accompaniment. Contrary to the generally held view that all baroque ensemble music includes the basso continuo, secular instrumental music throughout the period allowed for performance by single-line instruments alone.

Early seventeenth-century secular ensemble music consists chiefly of dances and pieces called sinfonias. The earliest publications group together pieces of the same kind: sinfonias, gagliards, correntes, etc., and it was evidently up to the performer to select pieces that could be performed as a suite. In his fifth book G.B. Buonamente (1629) suggests how this can be done by including what amounts to two small suites, each consisting of a sinfonia, a gagliarde, and a corrente, all in the same key. In Buonamente's seventh book (1637), Vincenti, the printer, explains that "each sinfonia has its brando, gagliarde, and corrente." Such groupings surely reflect a common practice. The chamber sonata consists of similar collections of dances, frequently with a sinfonia as the opening movement.

In the early seventeenth century the term "sinfonia" is attached to many different kinds of works. Within the context of dance collections, however, its meaning is quite specific. A sinfonia is a short, usually homophonic piece in binary form. The term is first encountered in Salomone Rossi's 1607 collection of sinfonias and gagliards in three, four, and five parts.

The sinfonias provide a crucial link between sixteenth- and seventeenth-century practice. Their ancestry is found, not in instrumental music, but in popular sixteenth-century vocal music, specifically the canzonetta. Joel Newman (1962, 122) observes that "the similarities in atmosphere, rhythmic procedure, texture, and format" are so striking that the sinfonias "may be considered textless canzonette of the binary type."

Rossi was the leading composer of secular instrumental music in the first decades of the seventeenth century and his three-part sinfonias provided a textural model for dance music. Sixteenth-century collections of dances are usually in four and five parts, and that is also true of the five gagliards included in Rossi's first book. Two of these, however, optionally could be performed by three instruments. The trio texture, commonly found in both vocal and instrumental music at the time, had obvious appeal. It is hardly surprising that all 18 dances included in Rossi's third book (1613) were in three parts, two trebles and bass. More importantly, this texture was accepted by other composers and by 1630 dominated the field of dance music.

The trio texture of the canzonette is harmonically complete, and the same is true of Rossi's trios as well as those by his contemporaries. Many dance collections make no mention of a basso continuo, and the performance by three single-line instruments was evidently intended. The three surviving books of secular instrumental music by G.B. Buonamente (1626, 1629, 1637) each have three printed parts for two violins and a bowed bass instrument. The texture may seem thin to twentieth-century ears, as is shown in a passage (ex. 1.6) from Buonamente's fourth book (1626). But the keyboard music by one of Buonamente's contemporaries, Martino Pesenti (1630), contains precisely the same kinds of textures (ex. 1.7), and there is reason to believe that the composer would have opposed the idea of enriching the texture. Pesenti's preface explains his use of dissonances, pointing out that their effect is best when not accompanied by the inner parts. His statement suggests that inner parts were supplied even in solo keyboard works, but that a thin texture nevertheless is preferable. In short, Buonamente's three-part pieces, which excluded the basso continuo, clearly fall within the boundaries of desirable textures at the time of their writing. There is no reason to believe that he intended his pieces to be performed by any other instruments than those mentioned in the titles, namely, two violins and a bass.

In this light it appears that Rossi's instrumental music also may have been intended for performance without a realization of the bass. His trios call for a chitarrone "or other similar instrument" (1613) and *stromento da corpo* (1607). None of his works specifies a basso continuo, though it is usually assumed that the chitarrone, being capable of realizing the bass,

Example 1.6.   G. Buonamente, *Gagliarda seconda*, 1626

Example 1.7.   M. Pesenti, *Corrente detta la granda*, 1630

would do so. The expression *stromento da corpo* may seem to suggest a function similar to Agazzari's (1607) "foundation instruments," which realized the bass. But a *stromento da corpo*—an "instrument with a body," or perhaps better, a belly—could equally well be a gamba or a cello (see chap. 13). Buonamente, who for years served in Mantua together with Rossi, calls for a *basso di viola* on the lower part in his dances, and it stands to reason that the two composers sought the same kind of performance. While the chitarrone was capable of providing a realization, there is a strong case for its having been used to play the bass line alone in much seventeenth-century music. Rossi's collections of instrumental music are one case in point.

Not all seventeenth-century dance music was performed with only a single-line instrument playing the bass. In a collection of dances published in 1642 Uccelini includes a basso continuo but no bass-line instrument. Other composers, notably Biagio Marini (1626), include parts for bass as well as for basso continuo. The practice was therefore highly pluralistic in allowing for three ways of performing the bass: (1) bass-line instrument alone, (2) chordal instrument alone, or (3) both together.

Because of the inconsistent terminology of the early seventeenth century it is frequently difficult to distinguish between music in the canzona tradition and music in the secular realm. The distinction can usually be made by considering the contrapuntal nature of the work in relation to the number of parts specified in the title.

The titles of sixteenth-century canzonette, like those of all other ensemble music at the time, reflected the number of voice parts. The three-part canzonette, of which there are many, were labeled *a tre*. Similarly, Rossi's sinfonias are labled *a tre*, as are his dances and those of other composers who use the trio texture. This practice differs significantly from that of the canzona and other works in the church sonata tradition. Here the principal parts mentioned in titles need to be of contrapuntal nature and take part in the imitations. Thus a *canzona a tre* would have three contrapuntal parts; a sinfonia *a tre*, being homophonic, would have only one melodically important part.

This difference in the way of referring to the parts provides a means for distinguishing between pieces in the canzonetta tradition and the canzona tradition, or in other words, between secular instrumental music and that intended for church. Such works sometimes are included in the same publications, as is the case with Marini's opus 8 (1626). The table of contents indicates the number of parts in each piece. If a movement *a tre* has three contrapuntal parts, it can be assumed to belong to canzona-church sonata tradition. If, on the other hand, the piece is homophonic, it belongs in the secular realm with dances and sinfonias.

Table 1.2. Instrumental Combinations in Italian Secular
Ensemble Music, 1670–1680

Duos
Violin and spinet	1
Violin, violone or spinet	3

Trios
Two violins and violone	1
Two violins, violone or spinet	5
Two violins, violone and spinet	1

Quartets, or Larger (only bass and continuo parts listed)
Bass part for violone or spinet	1
Separate parts for violone and basso continuo	3
Total number of works:	15

The *Sonata da Camera*

If surviving publications proportionally reflect the total printed, the years
1640–65 were lean as far as dance collections go; only nine titles are listed in
Sartori's bibliography (1952). Beginning in 1666 a sudden increase occurs;
on the average, two collections survive from each year (not counting
reprints). The apparent burst of activity coincides with significant changes
in the repertory associated with a new generation of composers, among
whom are Giovanni Battista Vitali (ca. 1644–92), Giovanni Maria Bononcini (1642–78), and Giuseppe Colombi (1635–94).

The collections contain dances organized according to key into what in
effect are suites. But the dances, in the past intended for the ballroom, are
in the process of moving into the drawing room. Vitali (1667) distinguishes
between pieces intended for dancing — *per ballare* — and for the chamber —
da camera. The same distinction is found in other works from this time. The
term "chamber sonata" arises, not in contradistinction to the church sonata,
but to distinguish actual dances from stylized ones. This repertory, while
maintaining the rhythmic vigor of the dance, increasingly tends toward
polyphony, and by the end of the century had acquired a texture of considerable contrapuntal complexity.

The collections of stylized dances, whether under the name of chamber
sonatas or not, are in important respects similar to the earlier collections of
dance music. Trio texture prevails, but other combinations of from two to
six instruments also occur. Table 1.2 shows the different combinations in
the secular works listed by Sartori (1952) and published between 1670 and
1680. The performance of the bass includes the three alternatives seen earlier in the century: bass-line instrument alone, basso continuo alone, or
both together. But there is an entirely new twist to the listing of alternatives.

No fewer than nine out of the fifteen works have the option of using either a bass instrument or a chordal instrument. Only one bass part is included, and nothing suggests that two instruments would be required for its performance.

Ensembles consisting of four or more instruments frequently include separate parts for violone and basso continuo. The violone part does not contain imitations and its presence is not the result of its contrapuntal importance. Rather, the large ensemble indicates a desire to create a rich sound, and both a bass and a basso continuo instrument are needed. The same tendency can be observed in other repertories for large ensembles, such the concerted sacred music and the incipient concerted music for instruments, with the same result as far as the employment of bass instruments is concerned.

Smaller ensembles normally use one instrument for the bass part. Of the eleven publications of duos and trios, only one has parts for both violone and spinet. One of the collections makes no mention of a chordal instrument at all and must have been intended for performance by bowed string instruments alone. In the case of duos and trios, the standard performance of dance music in the 1670s consisted of the bass parts being played by a bowed bass instrument or by a chordal instrument, but not by both at the same time.

The secular sonatas published in the 1690s differ in important respects from the dances of the 1670s. Binary form is no longer a given. More importantly, the principal parts have acquired greater contrapuntal independence, and that change includes the bass. This repertory benefits from the presence of a bass-line instrument, with or without the participation of a chordal instrument. A performance with the bass played by a chordal instrument alone might well have been considered less satisfactory than the two other alternatives.

Chamber Sonatas without a Chordal Instrument

Secular instrumental music is the only genre of Italian music in which the continuo is not obligatory and in which its performance by single-line instruments was considered satisfactory. Performance of the bass by a stringed instrument alone is specified in a number of manuscripts and publications from the latter half of the seventeenth century (Jensen 1980). The biggest problem in not using a chordal instrument comes in duos, where the texture may seem thin. That, however, was not of great concern, a point well illustrated in a collection of dances for violin and violone or spinet by G. M. Bononcini, published in 1671. In the dedication Bononcini points out that the violone is more appropriate for the bass part than the harpsichord.

Among those who preferred the exclusive use of bowed instruments, at least one questioned the thin textures in duos performed without a keyboard realization. T. Pegolotti, in his *Trattenimenti armonici da camera, a violino solo, e violoncello* (1698), suggests that the cellist may add some high notes in addition to the bass. It is important to realize that Pegolotti is not advocating the addition of a harpsichord, because this instrument is nowhere mentioned. The composer clearly wanted the sound of two stringed instruments, and if the sonority was wanting, the solution was not to add a keyboard accompaniment, but, rather, to make a partial realization of the bass on the cello.

F.T. Arnold (1931, 329) cites one case in which Veracini was accompanied only by a cello and goes to some length to explain that this must have been quite an exceptional occurrence. But in light of the many indications that chamber sonatas were performed without a chordal instrument, there is nothing unusual about Veracini's appearance with a cellist alone.

The most persuasive argument for taking the option "violone o spinetta" at face value is the fact that, in the publications employing that expression, the bass part is never referred to as the basso continuo in seventeenth-century sources. When a spinet is used it would obviously play a realization and, in fact, function as a basso continuo. But that would not apply to a violone, which would play the part as notated. The titles avoid any possibility of misunderstanding by mentioning the names of the instrument and avoiding any implication that the bass should be realized.

Works in which both violone and spinet are required normally refer to the keyboard part as the basso continuo. The same is true of the organ part in church sonatas. The expression "violone or spinet" therefore carries no implication that both instruments should be used.

Chamber Sonatas with Both a Chordal and a Bass-Line Instrument

The option of using "violone o spinetta," found in so much Italian baroque music, goes against present notions of basso continuo performance and has occasioned various attempts at explaining it away. In a widely quoted passage F.T. Arnold (1931, 329) argues that the expression really means "violone e spinetta," referring to works by Vivaldi and Valentini that use "o" in the title but "e" in the part. The assertion is certainly not valid for the seventeenth century because the option of using either a spinet or a violone is firmly rooted in the practice of that time. The two cases cited by Arnold, however, may be indicative of an increasing tendency to use both instruments in music written after 1700.

This tendency to use two instruments for the performance of the basso continuo goes together with a change in the meaning of that term. During the seventeenth century the term "basso continuo" always refers to a chordal instrument alone. In the early eighteenth century the term, at times, refers to a bass-line instrument as well as to a chordal instrument, for instance in Marcello's *Sonate a flauto solo con il suo basso continuo per violoncello o cembalo* (1712). The change in the meaning of the term may well be indicative of a change in the performance of the basso continuo that was about to take place.

A noticeable increase in the use of chordal instruments together with bass-line instruments occurs toward the end of the seventeenth century. Of the eight secular trios listed by Sartori (1952) from the years 1690–93, three include parts for both instruments. This is a significant increase when compared to the situation two decades earlier shown in table 1.2; at that time only one of eleven works had such parts. Moreover, around 1700 a case can be made for including both instruments in the absence of separate parts.

This development may be a result of influence from the church sonata. In fact, many of the chamber sonatas are church sonatas in disguise. The connection between the two genres is particularly well illustrated by Corelli's opus 5, popularly known as "solo sonatas" but entitled *Sonate a violino e violone o cimbalo* (1700). While the title sidesteps the issue of church or chamber, the use of the harpsichord indicates that the collection was intended for the chamber.

The sonatas fall into two groups, half of them modelled on the church sonata, and the other half modelled on the chamber sonata. Each "church sonata" contains at least one, but usually several movements, in which the bass is contrapuntally active. In such movements both the violin and the violone are indispensable, and the performance tradition of the church sonata demands that a chordal instrument be present as well.

The problem in including both a chordal instrument and a bass-line instrument in Corelli's opus 5 is that the work was published in score format so that all three performers would have to read from the same part. Indications are that this was not an uncommon practice. F.A. Bonporti's *Invenzioni a violino solo* (1712) was also published in score format and the title shows the need for three instruments: violin, cello, and harpsichord. G. A. Piani's *Sonate a violino solo e violoncello col cimbalo* (1712), also published in score, was, according to the title, intended for performance by three players. Though published in Paris, the work is of interest for Italian practices, given the indications in Bonporti's *Invenzioni*. These publications together suggest that the continuo and a bass instrument may both be included, even in the absence of separate parts. And though all the works cited are for solo violin with accompaniment, it would seem that the doubling of the bass would be applicable in works for three or more instruments as well.

One other work may have a bearing on the practice of having three players read from the same part: Porpora's *Sonate XII di violino e basso* (1754). Like the works by Bonporti and Piani, Bonporti's sonatas were published in score format. The dedication, in a parenthetical note, makes clear that the word "basso" in the title refers to two instruments: harpsichord and cello. This not only corroborates the indications by Bonporti and Piani but also suggests that two instruments are now expected to perform the bass part.

Porpora's work was published in Vienna, and its relevance to Italian practice is therefore uncertain. Perhaps the doubling of the continuo line was characteristic of music in the country of publication. If so, one may take Haydn's piano trios as illustrations of how the practice of bass-line doubling becomes embedded in the emerging Viennese style. The bass in these pieces is of no melodic interest, yet a cello is always included. The cello line and the bass of the keyboard part are usually identical and the trios constitute a classical case of bass-line doubling. Significantly, such clear-cut cases are not often found in works before 1750 unless the bass is a melodically significant part. This circumstance parallels the practice in sacred vocal music, where bass-line doubling becomes the practice in the last half of the eighteenth century.

Summary

Secular instrumental music for small ensembles shows an unusual variety in the performance of the bass during the entire baroque period. Unlike any other genre of Italian music, this repertory may be performed without the participation of a chordal instrument. The greater melodic independence given to the bass toward the end of the seventeenth century only enhanced the unaccompanied performance, which flourished well into the eighteenth century. But around 1700 one finds a distinct tendency to use both a chordal and a bass-line instrument, both players performing from the same part. The obligatory use of both instruments in chamber sonatas may have become a general practice around 1750 or later.

8

Conclusion to Part One

Basso Continuo Omitted

The principal concern in the preceding discussion has been the use of bass-line instruments and their relationship to the basso continuo in Italian baroque music. A more fundamental question worth considering for a moment is whether a basso continuo always should be present. F.T. Arnold (1931, xii), writing at a time when the continuo was left out of performances for frivolous reasons, points out that "there is not a single indication, in any one of the contemporary treatises on the subject, that the figured Bass accompaniment was ever regarded as, in any sense, optional." Throughout his book, Arnold argues as if the continuo always can be taken for granted. Arnold relies on treatises and does not fully take into account the significant number of musical sources showing that the continuo indeed was optional.

The absence of a chordal instrument would seem to be most appropriate in large ensembles where the harmony is complete, but that is not the case. A chordal instrument is least needed in secular instrumental music—dances and chamber sonatas in two and three parts. Many publications neither mention a chordal instrument, nor imply its use. Others allow the bass to be played by either a violone or a spinet, and either alternative was equally satisfactory.

Publications of sacred choral music consistently contain basso continuo parts, but these are sometimes optional. This is true of two early Roman publications by Agostino Diruta (1630) and Filippo Vitali (1641), and similar cases are found throughout the Italian baroque. It is doubtful, however, that instruments were dispensed with altogether. The title of Cazzati's *Salmi a 8,* opus 21 (1660a) tells that the work can be performed with two organs, one organ, or without. But a note to the reader indicates that in the absence of organ it is necessary to add some instrument, such as a violone or a trombone, "in order to stay on pitch." In that case, Cazzati adds, the tempo must be slower; apparently the more complete accompaniment of the organ made it easier to stay on pitch and maintain an appropriate tempo.

Sometimes composers deliberately leave out the continuo accompaniment. This commonly occurs in eighteenth century opera, sometimes for programmatic reasons (Cross 1981, 1:100; Kolneder 1973, 76). In Vivaldi's concertos the lowest part frequently drops out, and with it the continuo. This may affect as much as half of the music in this repertory (Kolneder 1973, 77).

Bass-Line Instruments in the Early Baroque Period

Contrary to twentieth-century notions, there is no general practice of doubling the continuo line with a bass-line instrument in the early Italian baroque period. The theoretical sources clearly imply that the continuo normally was performed by a chordal instrument alone. The performance material confirms this state of affairs, though the presence of parts for bass-line instruments in some genres may, on the surface, seem an indication to the contrary.

Vocal music dominates the early part of the seventeenth century almost as much as it did the sixteenth century. Whether sacred or secular, publications of vocal music before 1660 never include bass parts doubling the continuo, and the titles and prefaces contain nothing to suggest that such parts should be added. Descriptions of performances, mostly of secular songs, frequently mention performers accompanying themselves. Concerted sacred music sometimes includes a bass instrument, which, however, does not double the continuo, but supports the violins and rests when they do. A separate part is provided when bass instruments are needed, and there are no indications that the continuo player and the bass player ever read from the same part.

Instrumental music frequently contains parts for a bass-line instrument, but the function is not to double the continuo. A bass-line instrument is obligatory in canzonas and church sonatas when the part is contrapuntal. This fact is acknowledged in the title and a separate part is provided. Italian publications are consistent on this point, and apparent inconsistencies arise when publications in other countries are considered. In Purcell's *Ten Sonatas in Four Parts* (1697) the continuo counts as one of them, logical in terms of English seventeenth-century practice where the keyboard often handles several contrapuntally important lines. But in Italian publications of church sonatas the continuo is never counted as one of the principal parts.

The only seventeenth-century genres in which it may be appropriate to speak of bass-line doubling are opera and oratorio. The documentation is scantier than on any other genre, but it appears that the chordal instrument was supported by some bass instrument, such as the cello or one of the extended lutes.

Bass-Line Instruments after 1680

A number of developments around 1680 greatly affected the use of bass instruments. These are best summarized in terms of what happened in secular music for small ensembles on one hand, and in sacred music for large ensembles on the other.

In the chamber cantata and the chamber sonata the bass part became increasingly important, creating the need for a single-line instrument in addition to the continuo. The two players read from the same part, a necessity in the case of chamber cantatas, which invariably were written in score format. Using two players on the bass part was common but certainly not obligatory in the early decades of the eighteenth century.

The case for using both a continuo instrument and a bass instrument in secular music with a single bass part is based on the assumption that two players read from the same part. The earliest indication of this kind occurs in a collection of vocal music by Carlo Grossi from 1675 where the bass part is intended for cello and basso continuo. How far back such a practice extends is unclear, but if French practice has a bearing on the case it appears that Grossi's usage must have been something of a novelty. Dumont (1657), in a publication which provides parts for bass viol and harpsichord, points to the difficulty in using only one part. But by 1700 single parts for two players are common in France, the distinction between the two shown by the stems going in opposite directions (Sadie 1980, 30, 33).

In church music the rationale for including bass-line instruments with the continuo is entirely different than in secular music. The need arises, not from considerations of the melodic significance of the part, but from considerations of balance in large ensembles. This situation comes up in concerted vocal music and in the instrumental repertory intended for orchestral performance. The doubling of the bass is particularly noticeable in music published after 1680. Separate bass parts are always included, since a seated player of a bass instrument would have difficulties reading from the same part as the organist.

Separate bass parts also make their appearance in sacred music for solo voice and for choir. Such parts are found increasingly after 1700 in manuscripts and publications, though still very much in the minority.

During the first decades of the eighteenth century, then, bass-line instruments were frequently playing the same part as the continuo in many different genres of Italian music. The increased use of two instruments playing the same part is reflected in a change of the meaning of the expression "basso continuo." During the first two-thirds of the seventeenth century, basso continuo is synonymous with a chordal instrument or the part for such an instrument. The consistency of this usage is particularly well illustrated in chamber sonatas which include a single bass part for violone or spinet. Although the spinet would in fact function as the basso continuo, that expression is avoided since it would not apply to the violone.

The change in the meaning of basso continuo seems to have its roots in Bolognese usage in the last decades of the seventeenth century. The performance materials for the concerted music in the San Petronio archives contain two kinds of bass parts, one which plays intermittently and is part of the orchestra, the other continuous, doubling the continuo line. The two kinds of parts are designated respectively, *violone spezzato* and *violone continuo*. Occasionally the instrument is not specified and the part is called simply basso continuo.

Using the expression basso continuo to refer to the part for the bass-line instrument occurs in a variety of sources from around 1700. Colonna's *Psalmi ad Vesperas* (1694) contains parts for organ and *bassus continuus*, and such parts are also found in sacred vocal works by Bassani (1699, 1710) and Bernabei (1710). Marcello's recorder sonatas, opus 2 (1712), call for "Basso continuo per violoncello o cembalo." This terminology also appears in the theoretical literature. Z. Tevo, describing the instrumentation in large-scale concerted music for the church, says that the violoni and the theorbos play the basso continuo, not as a substitute for but in addition to the organ (Tevo 1705, 360).

It is doubtful that a general practice of doubling the basso continuo line ever developed in Italy during the baroque period. The reason for using a bass-line instrument in secular music was invariably the need to bring out a melodically significant line, but it is quite clear that performance with a keyboard instrument alone was fully acceptable under many circumstances.

Sacred music provides the best documentation of the use of bass-line instruments in that separate parts always are included when the instruments are needed. Such parts occur only sporadically in manuscripts and publications from the first half of the eighteenth century. Sometime after 1750 parts for cello and double bass become standard in sacred music of all genres. A practice of bass-line doubling in Italian music therefore seems to have developed not during the baroque period, but at a later time.

Bass and Basso Continuo: Who Doubles Whom?

At the heart of twentieth-century misconceptions about bass-line doubling is the notion that the basso continuo is the principal part. As a result, the presence of a bass instrument is by definition a doubling of the continuo.

When the bass part is the more animated of the two it is still not described as a principal part, but as a concertante version of the thoroughbass.

The view that the continuo is the principal part is not a historical fact but a modern interpretation of the stylistic changes that took place in Italy around 1600. The basso continuo, so the argument goes, first appeared in sacred choral music as a dependent part, arrived at by extracting the lowest sounding notes in the work to form a continuous line. Such a part is commonly, and incorrectly in terms of seventeenth-century usage, referred to as a "basso seguente."

The next important step, according to the argument, occurred with the appearance of monody, which differed from sacred music in having a freely composed bass. The basso continuo is by necessity an independent line because there are no other parts from which it could be derived. Since monody is one of the pillars of baroque style it follows that the independent continuo is the ideal in all genres of music.

The argument is misleading in focusing on the treble-oriented monody and ignoring the large repertory in which a vocal or instrumental bass is present. In sacred concertos for solo voices and in canzonas and church sonatas the bass is counted among the principal parts while the continuo is not. And the continuo is regularly a simplified version of the principal bass part. In choral music the continuo part is derived from the vocal parts. The voices may drop out momentarily so that the continuo is alone; that makes the accompaniment indispensable, but it does not make the continuo line as a whole melodically independent.

The method of constructing the basso continuo shows its lack of independence. Penna (1672, 129) describes how the continuo part is assembled, so to speak, after the process of composition is completed. The principal bass part, instrumental or vocal as the case may be, supplies most of the notes needed in the continuo. Where the principal bass has rests, the continuo part is formed by taking the lowest sounding note from the other parts. This process is precisely the same as used by organists in the late sixteenth century and the result in either case is a dependent part. Penna mentions both organ and spinet as the chordal instruments so that his description is relevant to the composition of sacred as well as secular music.

The subordinate character of the continuo is reflected in thoroughbass manuals throughout the baroque period. Fast motion may be left out when the principal bass part is sung or played, leaving only the harmonically active notes needed for the realization. The function of the chordal instrument is not to project the bass but to provide an accompaniment. The basso continuo part is not a melodic line but more like symbols showing which chords to play.

When a separate bass part is provided, vocal or instrumental, it is inappropriate to speak of the basso continuo being doubled. The bass instrument has the principal part from which the continuo is derived. The basso continuo doubles the bass, not the other way around. The bass part is obligatory and cannot be left out without substantially distorting the texture.

Nevertheless, the notion of doubling of the basso continuo, though frequently inappropriate, has validity in Italian music for large ensembles. Such doubling seems to have been practiced in opera and oratorio all through the baroque period. Outside opera, the doubling of the bass is associated with concerted music for the church, a development that gained momentum around 1680. As the performance forces grew larger the bass needed more support and a violone or a theorbo, or both, were added. Their purpose was clearly to strengthen the continuo, and the parts are usually identical, printed from the same plates. Under such circumstances it is quite appropriate to speak of doubling the basso continuo.

Part Two

The Bowed Bass Instruments

Introduction to Part Two:
Problems of Terminology

The Italian bowed bass instruments of the seventeenth century go under a confusing multitude of names: violone, viola, bassetto, violoncino, violoncello, and many others. Some of these change meaning in the course of time and from one region to another. The same term may refer to more than one instrument; conversely, the same instrument may go under several different names. Only four different instruments can be identified with certainty: the bass gamba, the double bass gamba, and two kinds of bass violins. Few specimens have survived, and those preserved have often been extensively altered. Since only a limited amount of documentary material is available, the area of seventeenth-century bowed bass instruments in Italy is wide open for divided opinions and elaborate theories.

The term "violone" without doubt causes the most complex terminological dilemma in that it was used for three of the four instruments just mentioned. Stephen Bonta (1977, 1978) argues that the term, after the first decade of the seventeenth century, refers to the bass violin. Alfred Planyavski (1970) holds that the term principally refers to the double bass. The view taken here is that during the seventeenth century in Italy the term refers mostly to the Italian bass gamba, and at times to the cello and the double bass.

9

The Term "Violone"

Early Use of the Term "Violone"

The term "violone" is commonly used in the sixteenth century as a synonym for "viola da gamba." This usage is encountered in the writings of prominent theorists such as Lanfranco (1532), Ganassi (1543), and Ortiz (1553). Ganassi and Ortiz, whose works are specifically addressed to the gamba player, use the word violone in the titles as well as in the texts of their books.

Ganassi, as other sixteenth-century theorists, tuned the lowest string on the bass gamba to D, but his description of how the instrument is played suggests that this tuning was less than ideal. Most performers transposed their parts up a fourth, which meant using the next string up. In effect, the instrument was played as if it were tuned a fourth lower than actually was the case (Brown 1973, 52–53). The purpose of the transposition very likely ' was to take advantage of the brighter sound of the higher strings.

Ganassi's practice provides a likely rationale for the downward shift in tuning so that the lowest string is G', a fifth below that of the instrument which today goes under the name of bass gamba. This tuning is described by Zacconi (1592, libro 4, cap. 56), Banchieri (1609a, 53–54; 1611, 97), Cerone (1612, 1058–59), and Praetorius (1619b, 2:25,44).

Violone is still used as a generic term at the beginning of the seventeenth century. A manuscript treatise by G. Prandi, dated 1606, has a fingering chart for violoni which includes space for soprano, tenor, and bass (I-Bc MS E.19, fol. 53 v.). Only the tenor tuning was completed, showing the lowest string as D. In other words, Prandi's bass would have used the lower tuning with the bottom string at G'.

The generic use of the term violone is still occasionally found around the turn of the century. Agazzari, while discussing the violone as an ornamenting instrument, finds it necessary to stress that he is talking about its use on the bass part: "The violone, when on the bass part, proceeds gravely" ([1607] Kinkeldey 1910, 219). In the same paragraph Agazzari mentions a number of other instruments but not the specific parts they play, yet makes a point of it with the violone. The comment must have been intended to clarify which size of violone he had in mind.

At the time of Prandi's and Agazzari's writings, however, the term violone was no longer used for treble instruments, but had become exclusively associated with the bass and the double bass members of the gamba family. The new terminology appears in Banchieri's *Conclusioni del suono dell' organo* (1609a). While the soprano and alto instruments are called simply "viole," the two lower instruments are called, in ascending order, *violone in contrabasso*, and *violone da gamba*. The latter is the bass used for ensemble playing with other instruments and voices, the *primo viola del concerto*. Both instruments feature normal gamba tuning in fourths with a third in the middle, the bass going down to G' and the double bass to D'.

Banchieri's view is of especial significance because it occurs in a description of a performance of one of his works. A few years earlier (ca. 1607) while in Verona, he had been asked to write a mass, a large-scale polychoral work with several instrumental choirs. He took special notice of the tuning of the instruments, and back in Bologna he consulted with a local musician on this matter (1609a, 50). The tuning and terminology would therefore seem to have been common both around Venice and around Bologna. The ensemble included a full complement of members of the violin family as well as of the gamba family. The lowest string on the bass violin was G (Banchieri 1609a, 55), too high for most bass parts. The violone had an appropriately low range and was designated as the principal bass instrument of the ensemble, a role that it was to maintain in much seventeenth-century music.

Praetorius (1619b, 2:25) also employs the term violone, not for the bass gamba but only for the double bass. He gives several tunings, one of them identical to Banchieri's. Praetorius's violone has been estimated to equal in size the modern double bass, which is 114 cm (Bessaraboff 1941, 361), and this presumably also holds for Banchieri's *violone in contrabasso*.

Banchieri's terminology, which distinguishes between the bass and the double bass violoni, is employed in early seventeenth-century sources. In 1614 the payment records at San Marco in Venice list a player of a *violone contrabasso* (Selfridge-Field 1975, 299) while the preface to Sigismondo d'India's *Le musiche e balli a quattro* (1621) mentions a *basso di violone* used at the first performance. Given that two sizes of instrument were used, the word "violone" by itself would be ambiguous so that the qualifier was added in each case.

At Santa Maria Maggiore in Bergamo the expression *violone basso* occurs a number of times up to 1630 (Bonta 1978, 10, 17). References to the double bass vary considerably and three different expressions are common: *violone grosso, violone doppio,* and *violone grande* (Bonta 1978, 13). When the word "violone" is used without a modifier it does on occasion refer to the double bass (Bonta 1978, 14), but more commonly to the bass. In 1602 one of the players was listed twice as playing three instruments, among them the violone. When he was rehired in 1614 the notary added "violone grande" to the list of three he already played (Bonta 1978, 9). It seems that violone in 1602 must have meant a bass instrument, and that the addition in 1614 refers to a different kind of violone, the double bass.

It has been suggested that the word "violone" in the seventeenth century primarily refers to the cello (Cowling 1975, 57–60; Bonta 1977, 76–81). The central argument is that the word "gamba" hardly ever occurs in seventeenth-century scores and that the instrument was no longer in use. But a violone was by definition a gamba and no qualifier was needed. When, on the other hand, Ghizzolo (Calvi 1624) in 1624 calls for a *violone da brazzo* the implication is that the suffix "da brazzo" was needed to show that he wants a bass violin rather than a bass gamba. And Ghizzolo's usage, encountered in a single piece within a collection of music by different composers, does not in any way match the authority of Banchieri's detailed description of the instruments he had available for his Verona performance.

The Violone in Contrabasso

Early seventeenth-century terms referring to the double bass usually identify the instrument as belonging to the gamba family, either by calling it a violone (with a proper modifier such as *grande*), or a *contrabasso da gamba* as does Monteverdi in *Il Combattimento di Tancredi e Clorinda* (1638). In *Orfeo* Monteverdi calls for *contrabassi di viola*, an expression that could refer to the gamba family as well as to the violin family, but he probably means the same instrument as before. No Italian theorist describes a double bass violin at this time and later sources imply that instruments of that size belong to the gamba family.

The double bass is often called a *violone grande* and sometimes a *violone grosso*, the term used at St. Mark's in Venice in 1669 (Selfridge-Field 1975, 302). The orchestra there apparently made little use of the instrument because references to the double bass are infrequent. The same was true at San Petronio in Bologna where the expression *violone grosso* is found as late as 1681 but then dropped (Bonta 1977, 80).

The inventories of instruments at the Medici court between 1640 and 1669 contain unique information on double bass instruments (Hammond 1975). In 1652 the collection contained five *violoni a sei corde grandi*, confirming that the double bass is of the gamba family and has six strings (Hammond 1975, 206). Later entries identify the instrument as *contrabasso di viola a sei corde* (Hammond 1975, 212–13). The most intriguing entries, however, describe a large (i.e., double) bass gamba from Cremona with four strings, *un basso di viola grande da gamba di Cremona a 4* (Hammond 1975, 210). Since the regular bass instruments invariably are listed as *basso di viola*, a *basso di viola grande* must be a double bass. This instrument has four strings, yet it is identified as belonging to the gamba family. Equally important, it is made in Cremona showing that the most prestigious makers of violins made double bass instruments belonging to the gamba family. Since the instrument first appears in the records among entries from 1658 it might have been purchased around that time. A somewhat later entry, probably of the same instrument, calls it "a violone with four strings," *un violone a quattro corde*. For reasons already stated it is unlikely that this is a regular bass instrument, more so since the Medici records use the word violone in conjunction with the double bass only.

Bismantova, in the 1694 addition to his treatise, does not mention a six-string double bass at all. The four-string version appears under two different names: *violone grande* and *contrabasso* (Bismantova 1978, 118). The latter term is by this time widely used, for example, in Roman records from the 1680s on (Hansell 1966, 398–403; Liess 1957, 160, 163), and in Bergamo from around 1692 (Bonta 1978, 15). The tuning of the double bass is described around 1750 as E'A'DG (Panerai 1967, 9). That may have been the seventeenth-century tuning as well, though we shall see that it was not the only alternative.

The *Basso di Violone*

Violone in seventeenth-century Italian usage refers to a non-transposing instrument in the bass range and only rarely to a double bass. Both instruments are used in Cazzati's sonata *La casala* from his opus 35 (1665), shown in example 2.1. The violone part is at times quite florid and hardly suitable for performance in the lower octave, while the slow moving part for the double bass duplicates the organ. The violone, as we have seen, was the standard instrument in church sonatas where the bass part always was played at notated pitch. It is the principal bowed bass instrument of the seventeenth century, though toward the end it increasingly faced competition from the cello, which eventually would dominate.

The terminology in Cazzati's opus 35 was widely used, for example in Bergamo and Rome. The double bass instruments are listed as contrabassi, and the bass instruments as violoni (Bonta 1978, 19; Hansell 1966, 398–403; Kirkendale 1967, 256, 360ff.). Bass violins are not mentioned at all. Venetian publications show that the violone is a bass, rather than a double bass, in making it interchangeable with the cello (which in Venice often is referred to as "viola" (see chap. 10). In short, the word "violone," by itself, in

Example 2.1.   M. Cazzati, *Sonata la casala*, Opus 35

seventeenth-century Italy, refers to a bass instrument, most often the Italian bass gamba, and only in exceptional cases does it stand for double bass.

Sixteenth-century composers allowed their music to be played by all sorts of instruments, and the absence of references to the violone is to be expected. After 1600 composers increasingly specify the instruments of their choice and those, of course, include the violone. It is first mentioned in C. Assandra's *Motetti*, opus 2, published in 1609, the year in which Banchieri (in *Conclusioni*) identifies the instrument as a bass belonging to the gamba family. G. P. Cima uses the term in 1610, and so does G. F. Capello in his *Lamentationi* of 1612. This work was published in Verona where Banchieri a few years earlier had used violoni in his polychoral mass described in the *Conclusioni*. Given that description and the generic use of the term "violone" up to about 1600 it seems beyond doubt that all these publications require the bass gamba tuned to G'.

The Bergamo records come close to verifying that the violone was a bass gamba. A bill identifies two replacement strings for a violone as *sol re* and *G sol re utt*. This translates to d and g, corresponding to the two upper strings of the bass gamba tuned to G' (Bonta 1978, 18). One could argue* that the instrument might have been a double bass violin where the top strings would have been D and G, but the fact that no verification that such an instrument even existed makes it an unlikely possibility.

A description by Giovanni Battista Doni (1640, 314–15) helps to clarify the size of the violone. His *violone panharmonico* was an experimental instrument capable of playing in tune in all the modes. Several were made for use in the theater. Doni was concerned that the instrument should be able to project in a large hall full of people when playing together with harpsichords with multiple stops. As a result his violone was made larger than normal, so large that it could rest on the floor while being played. The measurements given indicate a body size of 91.6 centimeters.† Table 2.1 shows how this compares with those of other bass instruments from that time.

Doni's instrument was considerably larger than the bass gamba in G',

---

* Bonta (1978, 18) argues that the strings must have been intended for a double bass. He rejects the possibility that the violone could have been a gamba on the grounds that this instrument was not used in church. Banchieri's description of the Verona performance, cited above, documents the use of the violone in church, and the instrument in question almost certainly was a bass gamba tuned to G'.

† The size of the *violone panharmonico* given by Doni is four *palmi* and one *dito*. One Roman *palmo* equals 22.43 centimeters, and one *dito* is one twelfth of one *palmo*; consequently, the size of the body was 91.6 centimeters.

Table 2.1.   Body Sizes of Bass Instruments

Bass viol in D (Italian tenor)	68.0 cm
Modern cello	74.0–76.0 cm
Praetorius's bass viol in G'	78.5–82.5 cm
Doni's *violone panharmonico*	91.6 cm
Modern double bass	112.0 cm
Praetorius's violone (*contrabasso da gamba*)	114.0 cm

Note: The estimates of the sizes of instruments described by Praetorius are taken from N. Bessaraboff (*Ancient European Musical Instruments*, Boston: Harvard University Press, 1941, p. 361). The estimates of average body sizes are taken from Bessaraboff and from S. Marcuse, *Musical Instruments: A Comprehensive Dictionary* (New York: Norton, 1964).

and the reason was to make the instrument heard in a large room. In the seventeenth century the violone was extensively used in large churches such as San Petronio in Bologna, and there might well have been a general tendency to increase its size beyond that given by Praetorius.

The presence of the bass gamba in seventeenth-century Italy has frequently been questioned on the grounds of two accounts suggesting that the instrument went out of use. The French viol player Maugars, who visited Rome in 1639, comments on the absence of good gamba players (MacClintock 1979, 121). His comments, however, are concerned with solo playing and not necessarily with ensembles performing in church. Moreover, bowed bass instrument may have been in short supply in Rome at that time. Maugars's descriptions of church performances mention large lutes but never any bowed bass instruments. Roman payment records suggest that the bass parts were played by large lutes until about 1660 when the violone starts to appear (Wessely Kropik 1961, 33). Maugars's observations suggest, therefore, that no bowed bass instruments of any kind were in use at the time of his visit.

The strongest argument against the presence of the bass gamba comes in a letter from Thomas Hill written during a visit to that country in 1657. He comments that "the bass-viol they have not at all in use, and to supply its place they have the bass violin with four strings, and use it as we do the bass viol" (Hill, Hill, and Hill 1902, 110n). Hill apparently saw no bass gambas, or, at any rate, no bass gambas of the kind he would have known in England. This instrument, tuned to D, was considerably smaller than the violone, tuned to G', and Hill may not have recognized the Italian version for what it was. In England the violone would have been considered a double bass, as in the case of the "greate dooble base" of Orlando Gibbons (Meyer 1946, 3, 153, 163–64) tuned to A' and in the same range and size as the Italian violone. Hill's statement is important for observing the presence of cellos but does not necessarily indicate an absence of the violone.

The violone, in fact, must have been available in large numbers at the time Hill was in Italy because it is mentioned in the vast majority of publications requiring a bass instrument. It shows up in inventories and is depicted in at least one painting, by Evaristo Baschenis (1617–77) (Baines 1977, 175). The painting includes several instruments: a violin, a large lute (probably archlute or theorbo; the neck is not visible), and a guitar, but dominating the canvas is a large bass gamba lying upside down. The latter has six strings, frets, a flat back, and is of a size corresponding to that of the violone. The instruments depicted were all popular at the time and are frequently mentioned in seventeenth-century dance collections. The exclusion of the cello suggests that the violone still was the principal bass instrument in ensemble music, as it had been since the time of Banchieri.

Bass violins, while uncommon at the beginning of the century appeared with increasing frequency after 1640 and coexisted with the violone in performances and instrument collections. Both instruments were well suited for playing bass parts, and the inventories at the Medici court between 1640 and 1669 hardly distinguish between them. Whether of the gamba or the violin family they were simply called *bassi di viola*. The distinction, when needed, was made in terms of the number of strings, a *basso di viola a quattro corde* being a cello, and a *basso di viola a sei corde* a gamba (Hammond 1975, 204). Most entries do not specify the number of strings, but the instrument with four strings is mentioned most frequently. That frequency might indicate a larger number of bass violins, but it could also mean that the violone was more common so that the four-stringed instrument needed special mention.

The Violone as Ripieno Instrument

During the last half of the seventeenth century the soloistic function of the violone was increasingly challenged by the bass violin. This agile instrument relegated the violone to a supporting function, a development well illustrated in the rich collection of performance parts at San Petronio in Bologna. The orchestra included both the violone and the cello; double bass players were occasionally hired but were not part of the permanent ensemble (Enrico 1976; Schnoebelen 1969, 42). The bass parts can be divided into several groups with different functions. Some double the basso continuo while others are part of the orchestra and only play with the upper strings. The orchestral cello parts often differ from the violone parts in being more active. The violone part, in addition to being slower, is also at times notated one octave below the cello. Evidently the part is played at pitch, but has been slightly changed in ways reminiscent of a double bass part (Schnoebelen 1969, 47).

A somewhat similar distinction between the cello and the violone part is found in Legrenzi's sonatas opus 8 (Venice, 1663; Bonta 1977, 81–82). That, in turn, may shed light on the practice at San Marco in Venice where Legrenzi was maestro di cappella (1685–90). At San Marco, as at San Petronio, the double bass is infrequently mentioned and the bass instruments are cello and violone. Though the performance material from San Marco is not extant the distinction in the use of the two bass instruments may well have been similar to that in Bologna. But this practice must have differed considerably from circumstances in Rome where double basses were used in large ensembles from the 1680s on (Hansell 1966, 398–403).

No Italian writer comments on the difference in function between the cello and the violone in orchestral playing, but Quantz's comments, though written in Germany in 1752, may have a bearing on the case. The cellist, in his view, needs two instruments, a smaller one with thin strings, and for ripieno playing a larger one with thicker strings. Using only the smaller instrument in large ensembles the accompaniment "would have no effect whatsoever" ([1752] Reilly 1966, 241).

The violoni at San Petronio and San Marco orchestra apparently fulfilled the same function as the larger cello did for Quantz. The violoni, designed for ripieno playing would have benefited from the increased size of Doni's *violone panharmonico*. If such enlarged instruments were made, they would come close to the size of a small double bass. This would explain their use as substitutes for double bass instruments described above.

As the cello became the preferred bass instrument what became of the violoni? It appears that the larger ones may have been converted into small double basses. The crucial document for this argument is Bartolomeo Bismantova's *Compendio musicale* (1978). Written in Ferrara in 1677, the treatise discusses some theoretical matters, and gives rules for playing several instruments such as flute, cornetto, and violin. In 1694 the author added two more instruments, the *violoncello da spalla* which will be discussed below, and the *contrabasso o violone grande*. Since the *violoncello da spalla* made its appearance on the Italian scene around 1690 it may well be that the author considered the contrabasso something of a novelty as well. Large orchestras, where the double basses were needed, developed in the last quarter of the century and by 1694 the instrument may have been common enough to deserve description.

Bismantova's double bass had four strings, and the fingering chart shows that it sounded an octave below the notation (1978, 118). Since the instrument was tuned in fourths and the highest string was G, the bottom string should have been E′. In that case, Bismantova comments, the string would be too thick. A thinner string was apparently used because the pitch was raised to G′. Considering that double basses tuned to D′ were described at the beginning of the seventeenth century, the higher tuning is peculiar, to say the least. It suggests that Bismantova's contrabasso was something other than the instrument described by Praetorius, which is of the same size as the modern double bass.

The bottom string of Bismatova's contrabasso, G', is the same as on the regular violone, and these instruments would be interchangeable on parts with a low range and modest compass. As the cello increasingly took over the role as principal bass instrument there would have been a surplus of violoni which might lend themselves to conversion into the kind of double bass described by Bismantova. Robin Bowman believes that this is precisely the kind of conversion that is described in a receipt from 1701 in the archives at Santa Maria Maggiore in Bergamo, though conceding that the language is far from clear (Bowman 1981, 352). Whether the conversion took place or not, it is an entirely plausible procedure in light of the tuning of Bismantova's contrabasso.

The similarity in range between the violone and Bismantova's double bass provides a rationale for how those terms became synonyms later in the eighteenth century. From being the principal bass instrument in the early seventeenth century the violone was relegated to a ripieno function as cellos became increasingly available. The ripieno parts were in certain respects similar to double bass parts and may at times have been played in the lower octave; some of the parts for violone at San Petronio never descend beneath G and there would hardly be any reason to place such restrictions on the compass other than to allow for a descending octave transposition. The ripieno parts, at any rate, were eventually abandoned in favor of genuine double bass parts. In that situation the violone would function as a double bass rather than as a bass instrument. And if the strings were wound with silver, the size of the bass strings might be reduced sufficiently to extend the range downward from G' to E'.

The Term "Violone" Referring to the Cello

One of the problems with the term violone is that, in addition to referring to both the bass and the double bass gamba, it also at times stands for cello. The 1729 edition of the prestigious Italian language dictionary *Vocabulario degli Accademici della Crusca* defines violone as "a low pitched, large viol, which also is called bass viol [basso di viola], and, when of smaller size, violoncello." The dictionary was published in Florence, so it is hardly surprising that the expression *basso di viola* is used in the same sense as in the seventeenth-century Medici inventories, to refer to bass instruments collectively regardless of the family to which they may have belonged (Hammond 1975). But the most telling point is that the cello at times went under the name violone.

The use of the term violone to refer to the cello is particularly well documented in Rome. A change around 1720 in the record-keeping at the Ottoboni household makes violoncello the normal term for bass instruments which up to that time had been called violoni (Hansell 1966, 398–403). It is unlikely that all the players suddenly changed instruments. Perhaps genuine violoni prevailed when the record-keeping started so that the change to "violoncello" simply indicated that this instrument now was in the majority.

But it is also possible that violone was a specifically Roman term for cello. This usage goes back as far as 1650, to Kircher's *Musurgia universalis* (486) which contains a picture of a cello with the caption "violone." Bowed bass instruments were not used in Roman churches before 1660 (Wessely Kropik 1961, 33). The violone starts to be mentioned in the 1660s, at the time when bass violins increasingly became available. Whereas payment records speak of violoni and only rarely of violoncelli, the latter were conspicuously used, for example in Stradella's oratorio *San Giovanni Battista* (I-Bc MS BB.361) which was performed in Rome in 1675. And it stands to reason that the Roman proponents of virtuoso string music led by Corelli would have preferred the agile cello over the violone. Corelli's publications of chamber music followed tradition in calling for violone, yet that may have had a different ring to Roman than to Bolognese ears.

Outside of Rome, however, it is doubtful that the term violone referred to the bass violin until sometime after 1700. Before that time only three instances are known: a single piece by Ghizzolo in a collection of sacred music (Calvi 1624), Cazzati's opus 15 (1654), and Vitali's opus 2 (1667). In each case the word violone is followed by the qualifier "da brazzo." Without the qualifier the word violone during the seventeenth century referred to the Italian bass gamba tuned to G′.

10

The Bass Violin

The Small Bass Violin

The difficulty in discussing the violone is primarily that a single term may refer to a number of instruments different in size and belonging to different families. With the bass of the violin family the problems are quite different in that a multitude of terms refers to instruments in different sizes and with different tunings. Like all members of the violin family, the bass is tuned in fifths. The instrument came in two sizes: a small one tuned to F or G, and a large one tuned to B′ flat or C.

The small bass violin, originally tuned to F or G, has been virtually ignored since the time it went out of use. The instrument was the principal bass of the violin family in the early part of the seventeenth century. This fact explains why the violone became the dominating bowed bass instrument at that time: the bass violin simply did not have suffficient range in the low register. As larger bass violins became available after the middle of the century the smaller version was recycled and surfaced under new names such as *bassetto* and *violoncello da spalla*.

The bass violin tuning in F is mentioned by Cerone in 1612 and again in 1619 by Praetorius, who gives it as an alternative to the one in C. But the most important document for understanding the role of the bass violin at this time is Banchieri's *Conclusioni*, specifically the description, cited above, of the instruments that participated in the Verona performance around 1607. The violone is singled out as the principal bass instrument of the ensemble, *prima viola del concerto*, and for the obvious reason that it alone has the necessary range to cover a normal bass part. The bass violin, the *primo violino per il basso*, tuned to G, is not a true bass instrument and one can only speculate on what its function might have been (Banchieri 1609a, 53–54).

In the 1611 edition of *L'organo suonarino* Banchieri keeps the same tunings as in the *Conclusioni* but uses a slightly different terminology. The violin family is now called *violette da brazzo* (Banchieri 1611, 97), at the time a well known expression used in 1533 by Lanfranco (137) and again by Cerone in 1613 (1057). Banchieri calls the treble instrument "violino" so that only the alto and bass are called violette. This nomenclature must have been widely accepted because when the *L'organo suonarino* was reissued in 1628 with a new preface, no changes were made in the tunings or terminology. Another edition appeared in 1638, four years after the author's death, testifying to the popularity of the work and, perhaps, to the currency of its contents.

After Banchieri the smaller bass violin tuned to G is depicted in Kircher's *Musurgia universalis* (1650, 486). It may also be the instrument mentioned in the Medici inventories from about this time. Two entries in identical language, one from 1654 and another from 1669, list "three *bassi di viola*, two with four strings, and a similar smaller one" (Hammond 1975, 207, 215). The three instruments with four strings must have been bass violins of the regular size and the smaller one very likely a bass violetta.

References to the bass violetta in musical publications are rare. That is not surprising, given its limited range. But one might expect to find the instrument mentioned now and then, and that in fact is the case. It shows up in Dario Castello's sonatas of 1621, a work reprinted in 1629 and 1658. Only four of the sonatas have bass parts and three of these are for bassoon. The fourth sonata optionally calls for either a trombone or a violetta. The part is notated in baritone clef and goes to A. While exceeding the range of the alto and tenor violins, the part fits the range of Banchieri's bass violetta tuned to G. The reprint of 1658 suggests that the small bass violin as well as Castello's terminology were current at that time.

The small bass violin is also probably the instrument Marini had in mind when he asked for a *bassetto o viola da gamba* in the *Sonata sopra la Monica* from opus 8 (1626). The mention of the gamba as one possibility suggests that the bassetto is of a different family and that this instrument must be a bass violin. The part, like that for Castello's violetta, goes down to A, and it seems likely that the same instrument was intended in either case.

The bass violetta shows up again several times in the 1670s, for instance in some of the manuscript parts at San Petronio in Bologna. In Perti's psalm *Letatus a 3*, dated 1678, the violetta part follows along with the violone and the organ (Schnoebelen 1969, 53). Cherici uses the term violetta on the bass part of his opus 1, published in 1672 (Bonta 1978, 30).

At this time the term violetta is abandoned. Instead, Cherici in his opus 2 (1681) uses Marini's term *bassetto* and for obvious reasons. By 1670 violetta had become a standard term for alto violin and calling the bass by the same name created confusion. The problem was easily avoided by using the term bassetto, or *bassetto di viola*, a diminutive of *basso di viola* which properly described the difference in size between the two kinds of bass violins.

It appears that the term bassetto, having replaced violetta around 1670, was itself replaced by the expression *viola da spalla* about twenty years later. The bassetto is mentioned in publications from nearly every year between 1674 and 1687, again in 1693,and then virtually disappears except in reprints (Bonta 1978, 31). At this time the *viola da spalla* shows up prominently in the records at San Marco in Venice, being mentioned first in 1688, and again in 1689, 1690, and 1692 (Selfridge-Field 1975, 304). Since "viola" in Venetian usage is synonymous with "bass violin" it stands to reason that the *viola da spalla* belonged to the violin family. It is surely the same instrument that Bismantova calls a *violoncello da spalla* (1978, 118).

Bismantova's treatise was written in 1677, but seventeen years later he found it necessary to add descriptions of two instruments that apparently had become popular in the intervening years: the contrabasso, discussed above, and the *violoncello da spalla*. The tuning of the *violoncello da spalla* is nearly the same as that of the modern cello except for the lowest string, D, which is one whole step higher. This tuning may indicate that the strings were too short to produce the tension required to go down to C. The name, *violoncello da spalla*, points in the same direction, suggesting that the instrument was small enough to be carried over the shoulder (= spalla).

Bismantova's choice of the term *violoncello da spalla* is revealing when considered in light of local terminology in Ferrara, where he lived. The two Italian composers who most frequently call for the bassetto after 1670 were Mazzaferrata and Cherici, both residents of Ferrara. One might have expected Bismantova to mention an instrument prominently used by the two leading composers in town. Instead he speaks of a similar instrument which he calls a *violoncello da spalla*. The circumstances suggest that the two instruments are the same. By the time of writing, 1694, the term bassetto had become obsolete and Bismantova used the current expression *violoncello da spalla*. This conclusion is supported by considerations of range: the lowest string on the *violoncello da spalla* is D, and that is the lowest note ever required in parts for the bassetto (Bonta 1978, 29).

At the beginning of the seventeenth century the small bass violin was tuned to F or G and was clearly not suitable for most bass parts. With the invention of the silver wound string, the range could be extended downward to D, making the small bass violin a genuine bass instrument. Its agility, because of smaller left-hand reaches, must have been a considerable asset, though the smaller size was a liability in terms of volume and tone quality. The small bass violin helped to highlight these problems, and in so doing may have been a factor in the development that led to the reduction in size of the large bass violin toward the end of the seventeenth century.

The Large Bass Violin

The large bass violin, later known as the violoncello, is mentioned in the sixteenth century but ignored by early seventeenth-century Italian theorists in favor of the smaller bass discussed above. The absence of the large bass violin from theoretical treatises is matched in musical publications. Title pages frequently list a number of instruments suitable for the bass part, including the trombone, bassoon, chitarrone, and violone, but except as noted, not the bass violin. When Cavalli in his *Musiche sacre* (1656) calls for that instrument (under the name of *violoncino*), the printer, apparently concerned that the instrument might not be available, added a note explaining that any bass instrument capable of playing fast enough would do. The payment records at San Marco in Venice show no bass violin players until 1644 (Selfridge-Field 1975, 301); at Santa Maria Maggiore in Bergamo a cellist is first mentioned in 1653 (Bonta 1978, 24).

Because very few instruments have survived, one may speculate that few large cellos had been made up to this time. There are no records of sixteenth-century luthiers making cellos in large numbers as they did in the case of violins and double basses. If large bass violins were in short supply the situation was exacerbated by the plague of 1630–31 which took a heavy toll among violin makers in Cremona. Business there started to pick up around 1640, about the time when bass violins made their appearance in payment records and publications.

Even if rarely mentioned, some large bass violins were probably available. It may well be the instrument that Ghizzolo had in mind when, in 1624, he prescribed a *violone da brazzo* in one of his motets (Calvi 1624). A generation later Cazzati, in his opus 15 (1654), called for a *basso violone da brazzo*, probably referring to the same instrument.

After 1650 the presence of the bass violin is more easily documented because it acquired a name, or rather, several names of its own. After his opus 15 Cazzati switched from the cumbersome *basso violone da brazzo* to a single word, *violoncino*, which he used with some frequency while at Bergamo from 1653 to 1657. This term was first used in 1641 in a collection of instrumental music by G. B. Fontana and then occasionally until it disappeared around the turn of the century. The modern term, violoncello, first appeared in 1665 in a work by Arresti but did not gain currency until the 1680s (Cowling 1975, 59).

Venetian terminology with regard to the bass violin differed significantly from that of the rest of Italy. Two terms are common: *viola da brazzo* and simply *viola*. At the Conservatorio dei Mendicanti the inventories between 1661 and 1705 list the *viola da brazzo* as the bass instrument (Bonta 1978, 32–33). This expression is also found in published bass parts, for example in Giovanni Legrenzi's opus 8, which appeared in Venice in 1663.

The other term, viola, is used extensively in the employment records at San Marco and in a number of publications by composers from the Venetian territories (Selfridge-Field 1975, 301–5; Bonta 1978, 35–36). Several Venetian publications include the option of using *viola o violone* (Bassani 1691; Bonporti 1701) a clear indication that the term violone in Venice refers to a bass instrument and not to a double bass, as sometimes is claimed (Bonta 1978, 34).

The large bass violin was in the sixteenth century tuned to B′ flat. This tuning is implied by Lanfranco (1533, 137) and is mentioned by Jambe de Fer (1556, 63). It is mentioned again by Zacconi in 1592 (book 4, chap. 56).

K. Marx holds that the C tuning was established in Italy by 1610, and this view is widely accepted (Marx 1963, 45; Grove 1980, 3:806). His argument is based on a detailed study of the string parts in Monteverdi's *Orfeo*. Marx observes that the upper stringed instruments never ascend more than a diminished fifth above an open string and reasonably assumes that this must have been the case with the bass violin as well. Since the highest note in the bass part is d′, an instrument tuned to B′ flat would not do since a diminished fifth above the top string, g, would be a c′ sharp, one half step short of what is required. It seems at best questionable to take this as a fully satisfactory proof of the use of the C tuning, but that is a moot point. Bessaraboff (1941, 299) argues convincingly that the cello required in Monteverdi's *Orfeo* is tuned to G and that the lower notes were played by the bass gamba. Marx dismisses this view on the ground that the part goes down to C, a note not available on the bass gamba, he claims, having in mind the northern bass tuned to D (Marx 1963, 45–46). But the Italian bass gamba, the violone, goes down to G′ and would cover the entire range needed.

Important testimony to the continued use of the B′ flat tuning around the middle of the seventeenth century is found in G. Zanetti's *Il scolaro . . . per imparare a suonare di violino et altri stromenti*, published in Milan in 1645. The work consists of dances in four parts with tablature and musical notation on facing pages. Even with the B′ flat tuning shown by the tablature, the bass part never goes below C. This contradicts the commonly held view that the range of seventeenth-century bass parts indicates the tuning of the lowest string on the bass violin (Bonta 1977, 68). Zanetti's work illustrates the problem with this line of reasoning, as do the contemporary violone parts where not only the lower notes but even the lowest string is rarely used.

The low tuning may have been current as late as 1778 because B′ flat occurs in M. Bononcini's opus 12, published that year. While the title calls for violone, the part book is marked "violoncello," the first example of the author's using this term. The violone would of course have been able to play the B′ flat, but if the composer meant the part to be equally well suited for the cello, the lowest string must have been tuned to that pitch.

Pressure for changing the size and the tuning of the cello came around 1680. The most demanding repertory up to that time had been the church sonata. The obbligato bass parts were normally assigned to the violone but would have been suitable for the low-pitched cello as well. This repertory continued to evolve gradually and presented few problems for the bass player. The innovations came in the operatic repertory where the basso obbligato aria, which emerged at this time, made unprecedented demands in terms of agility and range, commonly going as high as f′ or even g′ (see chap. 5). The new type of aria soon found its way into the solo cantata repertory and even into church music, thereby creating new demands for highly accomplished performers on the bass violin in both sacred and secular music.

The appearance of virtuoso cellists testifies to the newly gained prominence of the instrument (Vatielli 1927, 119–48). Best known is D. Gabrielli (ca. 1650–90), a much sought-after performer and composer who lived in Bologna and whose operas were performed as far afield as Venice. His operas contain a number of arias with demanding cello parts.

Gabrielli's fame as a composer rests primarily on his *Ricercari*, the earliest known solos specifically intended for cello. Several of these pieces require the tuning CGdg in order for the double stops to be playable. It seems as if Gabrielli had abandoned the B′ flat tuning in favor of the one in C, while writing a few pieces in scordatura with the top string down one whole step. The score, however, contains no indications of scordatura and the somewhat peculiar tuning may have been intended in all the pieces. This procedure would make sense if Gabrielli used a large cello normally tuned to B′ flat. The biggest problem with this instrument is that the tension on the bottom strings is too low to produce a good sound (Bonta 1978, 5). Raising the pitch one step improves the sound but creates another problem: the top string, as on most stringed instruments, is already stretched to the limit. Leaving it at pitch while raising the three lower strings one step arrives at Gabrielli's tuning, one that considerably improves the sound of the instrument.

The irregular tuning, however useful at the time, was no permanent solution. The bass violin was expected to handle a higher tessitura than before and it was clearly desirable to raise the pitch of the upper string as well. To do so meant to reduce the length of the string by making the instrument smaller, thereby compromising the lower register again. But reducing the size held another attraction: it would diminish the left-hand reaches and make the instrument easier to play. The conflicting demands of making the instrument smaller while at the same time getting a good sound from the bass appear to have been reconciled by the invention of silver wound strings. This innovation allowed the size of the instrument to be reduced while not compromising the sound of the bass.

The reduction in the size of the cello is frequently associated with Stradivari who in 1707 started to make instruments with a body size of about 75 centimeters as compared to the previous size of about 80 cm. E. Cowling (1975, 32) cites the opinion of the Hill brothers who believed that the smaller cello was created by Andrea Guarneri between 1690 and 1695, a date that would fit well into the scenario suggested above. The B' flat tuning would therefore have been current in Italy until about the end of the century and the higher tuning came into general use on the cut down version of the large bass violin from its introduction around 1690.

Summary

The history of the bass violin goes back to the sixteenth century, but for a hundred years or more the instrument played no conspicuous role in Italian music. It is rarely mentioned before the middle of the seventeenth century, but from then on it gradually gains prominence.

The bass violin in early seventeenth-century Italy came in two different sizes: a large instrument tuned to B' flat, and a smaller instrument tuned to F or G. The theorists describe only the smaller instrument, which is occasionally used in compositions with a suitable compass. The larger instrument is rarely mentioned, and that may be the reasons why the violone, by the middle of the century, had become the most widely used bowed bass instrument.

The large bass violin is increasingly used after 1650 and plays a prominent part in the opera orchestra. The small bass violin is occasionally mentioned in bass parts, but the fortune of that instrument appears to have changed dramatically around 1670. The introduction of silver wound string extended its range down to D, making it a genuine bass instrument. During the last three decades of the century the small bass violin is frequently mentioned, first under the name bassetto, and later *viola* (or *violoncello*) *da spalla*.

Toward the end of the century the large bass violin was given florid parts with increasing frequency. The small bass violin had demonstrated the advantages of a smaller size instrument in music that require agility. This may have been among the reasons why the size of the large bass violin was reduced toward the end of the seventeenth century. Tuned a step higher than before, CGda, the large bass violin with a body size reduced from ca. 80 cm. to ca. 75 cm. is the instrument presently known as the cello.

Part Three

The Extended Lutes

11

The Instruments

Introduction

The extended lutes, little known today, played an important but poorly understood role in the baroque era. They were employed in vocal as well as instrumental music, in the chamber as well as in church. Usually thought of as continuo instruments, the extended lutes had a variety of functions, the most important of which may have been to play the bass line alone.

The extended lutes differ from the regular lute in that the bass range has been enlarged by the addition of up to eight unfingered strings commonly known as contrabassi. To accommodate the longer open strings the neck is extended to include a second peg box — one each for the fingered and the unfingered courses. These instruments are known under a variety of names: chitarrone, arciliuto (archlute), tiorba (theorbo), and others.

The study of the extended lutes has been made difficult by conflicting information in early seventeenth century sources and by the fact that the instruments were in a state of change at that time. Recent studies by Robert Spencer (1976), Douglas Alton Smith (1979), and Kevin Bruce Mason (1983) have provided much-needed clarification, particularly of the terminology. Two types of extended lutes are recognized: the theorbo, which in the early part of the seventeenth century went under the name chitarrone, and the archlute.

The Archlute

The archlute is basically a regular lute with added open strings on the extended neck. The instrument had 13-14 courses, of which 6-8 were stopped. The whole instrument might be double strung but at times the first course and the bass strings were single strung. Like the renaissance lute the archlute was tuned in G, a step below the most common tuning of the theorbo (ex. 3.1). Alessandro Piccinini (1623) claims to have invented the archlute in 1594 and his claim is generally accepted. Piccinini traces the

Example 3.1.   Tunings of the Extended Lutes

Tuning of the Archlute

Tuning of the Theorbo

ancestry of the instrument to the lute, and rejects the term *liuto attiorbato* — "theorbized lute" — on the ground that it erroneously suggests a kinship to the theorbo. In the seventeenth century the instrument is sometimes referred to simply as *liuto*, or *leuto*.

The gut strings employed on the archlute produce a rather soft sound. When covered strings came into use, sometime after the middle of the seventeenth century, the volume of the archlute was considerably increased. That may be the reason why the instrument is called for with some frequency in sources after 1680 while it is hardly mentioned in the preceding three or four decades. Now able to hold its own in terms of dynamics, the archlute had a distinct advantage over the theorbo in ease of playing and was probably preferred where speed was of importance.

The Chitarrone

The chitarrone was probably invented around 1588 by Antonio Naldi, a lutenist employed at the Medici court (Smith 1979, 445–47). It is used with considerable frequency in the Florentine *Intermedii* of 1589. By 1600 the term *tiorba* was used as a synonym for chitarrone by Cavalieri (1600) and other Italians soon follow suit (Mason 1983, 4). Chitarrone is the prevailing term in the early part of the century, while *tiorba* is preferred after about 1640.

The chitarrone differs from the archlute in several respects. The body is distinctly larger. Surviving specimens from the early part of the seventeenth century suggest that a stopped string on the archlute measured between 55–64 cm, while on the theorbo it might be as much as 90 cm (Grove 1980, 1:555).

Compared to the archlute, the strings on the theorbo are longer and require higher tension when tuned to the same pitch. This problem is exacerbated by the theorbo being tuned one step higher than the archlute, and the result is that the top two strings have to be tuned down one octave (ex. 3.1). The larger size also makes for larger left-hand reaches, which in turn affect the playing technique. Rapid passages are more difficult than on the archlute and block chords are awkward to play, so arpeggios are favored.

The chitarrone normally had fourteen strings, six on the fingerboard and eight open courses. The stopped strings are tuned like those on the lute, in fourths with a third in the middle, and the open strings descend diatonically another octave. The exact pitch level of the instrument is somewhat uncertain. Seventeenth century sources give either a' or g' as the top string but the size of surviving instruments suggests that other pitch levels may have been used as well (Mason 1983, 7–8).

The chitarrone always had single bass courses, while the stopped courses may have been either single or double. Theoretical and pictorial evidence indicates single stringing throughout. Surviving specimens, on the other hand, sometimes show double strings for the stopped courses, so both arrangements appear to have been used (Mason 1983, 6).

12

The Extended Lutes in
Italian Baroque Music

Though the archlute and the theorbo are similar in many respects, the two are not necessarily interchangeable. Most of the time the theorbo was preferred over the archlute. In the early seventeenth century both instruments were used for continuo accompaniments, but the theorbo is mentioned more than twice as often as the archlute. In the middle of the century the archlute is hardly mentioned at all but after 1680 it gains greater prominence than at any previous time.

From its earliest appearance in the 1589 Florentine *Intermedii* the theorbo was associated with accompaniment and ensemble playing. The instrument was called a chitarrone, a word probably derived from *cithara* (Spencer 1976, 409–10). The choice of an old Greek term may well have been a result of the interest in music of antiquity. This interest lies behind the creation of monody, and it is hardly coincidence that the primary use of the chitarrone was in works in the new style. After 1600 the chitarrone became one of the most popular instruments for the accompaniment of monodies; it is mentioned in nearly half of the 220 collections containing such pieces in the period 1600–35 (Mason 1983, 27, 119–36).

The chitarrone apparently has an advantage over the lute and the archlute in playing accompaniments. Giustiniani ([1628] MacClintock 1962, 79) says that the instrument is "more suitable [than the lute] for singing even moderately well and with a poor voice," and that it has been "eagerly accepted in order to avoid the great amount of labor needed to learn to play the lute well."

It seems strange that the chitarrone should be easier to play than the lute. The larger size, resulting in larger stretches, would, if anything, make the left-hand technique more difficult. Both instruments have open strings in the bass, and neither one would have an advantage on that score.

The attractiveness of the chitarrone for performers of monodies may have had something to do with the sound of the instrument and the manner of playing. Piccinini (1623, Cap. XXIX) illustrates how chords on the the chitarrone are always arpeggiated, even in the absence of any sign to that effect. Block chords are only used in fast pieces. Piccinini's comments are made in the discussion of solo playing, but the arpeggiation is apparently idiomatic to the instrument and therefore applicable to accompaniments as well.

The second advantage of the chitarrone is that the large size produces a fuller sound than does the archlute. That, in conjunction with arpeggios, may have helped to keep the sound alive in prolonged chords, which occur with some frequency in the monodic repertory.

Caccini, in his *Nuove musiche* ([1601] Strunk 1950, 56), speaks of the importance of the soloist not having to accommodate himself to others, implying that the singer also plays the accompaniment. The rhythmically free style of performance requires a flexible accompaniment, and the arpeggiated performance and sonorous open strings would be of great help in these matters. Caccini and others point out that the chitarrone was particularly appropriate for the accompaniment of the tenor voice (Mason 1983, 32-33). The reason is probably that the two upper courses are tuned down an octave so that the realization lies in a low register.

Within the monodic repertory the chitarrone is particularly well suited for the neoclassical music, i.e. the pieces in arioso and recitative style. Around 1620 strophic songs, often based on dance rhythms, increasingly gained popularity. Such pieces often call for guitar accompaniment, and the chitarrone is less well suited for this more animated repertory. As the neoclassical tradition faded away, so did the instrument associated with the origin of that style. After 1635 the chitarrone rapidly disappeared from publications; it is last mentioned in 1659 in a reprint of a collection of dances by Cazzati.

The disappearance of the term chitarrone does not mean that the instrument went out of use. Rather, it was from then on referred to by its other name: *tiorba*. Together with the change in terminology went a change in the repertory in which the instrument was used, and in the kind of part it played. With increasing frequency the theorbo was found in church sonatas, sacred vocal music, chamber sonatas and collections of dance music. It is normally mentioned as one of two or more instruments that may be used on the bass part, the other alternatives being bassoon, violone, bass violin, etc. The theorbo is rarely mentioned in continuo parts, not even as a substitute for another chordal instrument.

While the theorbo reigned supreme in the middle of the seventeenth century, the archlute led an obscure existence until about 1680. At that time the archlute asserted itself in both secular and sacred music, its new vitality probably caused by the introduction of silver wound strings and the resulting increase in volume. The superior agility makes the archlute preferable to the theorbo in certain repertories, but both instruments remain in use. The archlute is particularly often mentioned as an alternative to the violone on bass parts in church sonatas, and it is in this repertory that its agility may have offered the greatest advantage over the theorbo. The theorbo was especially favored in sacred vocal music where the archlute is rarely mentioned.

These are not the only uses of the extended lutes, however. In the opera orchestra the archlute is sometimes mentioned as the chordal instrument, substituting for the harpsichord. A few arias have written-out obbligato parts for the instrument. The archlute may also have been used as a continuo instrument in secular vocal music at this time; it is mentioned as an alternative to the harpsichord in the preface to Gasparini's cantatas opus 1 (1695).

13

The Extended Lutes as
Bass-Line Instruments

The extended lutes are generally thought of as chordal instruments and when used in baroque music the assumption is that they play a realization of the bass. This assumption is maintained in spite of contrary indications. The extended lutes are frequently given a regular bass part while a keyboard instrument plays the continuo. Moreover, the lute is almost always mentioned as being interchangeable with another single-line instrument such as violone, bassoon, or bass violin, but not with the chordal instrument. Obviously, the premise that the extended lutes always function as chordal instruments needs to be examined.

There are several reasons why the extended lutes are associated with continuo realizations. The early use of the theorbo for accompaniment certainly points in that direction. Another reason is the traditional view of the function of bass parts in baroque music, a subject dealt with at length in part one of this book.

The traditional and erroneous notion that the basso continuo is doubled by a single-line instrument implies that the latter in effect is part of the continuo. If so, it seems logical that chordal instruments included in the "continuo group" should all play realizations. But in reality the bass parts are separate from the continuo and are included because of a need to project the bass line as an independent part. Thus there is a solid musical reason for the player of the bass instrument, even an extended lute, to concentrate on the bass line itself but there is no need, nor a convincing rationale, for adding a second realization.

The extended lutes may be considered chordal instruments if that only means they are capable of playing chords. The theorbo, however, in spite of its wide use for accompanying monodies, is not well suited for continuo playing. With the two upper strings tuned down an octave the realization is too low for treble voices and instruments. The widely spaced frets make chordal realizations difficult to play, so arpeggios are substituted. Such broken chords are suitable for the accompaniment of a single voice but tend to get lost in an ensemble. The theorbo is simply not an effective continuo instrument and would add little in a piece where the organ or the harpsichord is already playing a realization. Significantly, when the extended lutes are called for to play the bass, the instrument mentioned is normally the theorbo, not the archlute.

Not only are the extended lutes ineffective in ensemble music when playing a realization in addition to that of the keyboard instrument: they also create intonation problems. G. B. Doni (ca.1635, 1: 111) observes that

> those who play the [arch-] lute or the theorbo together with organs and harpsichords always employ diminutions, because if they should use full chords, the discord would be recognized, whereas in a fast tempo, dissonance gives no trouble as it is not discernible.

> [quelli che suonano il Liuto, o Tiorba con gli Organi, o Clavicembali, sempre diminuiscono, perche se usassero botte piene, vi si conoscerebbe la dissonanza, la quale in note veloci non da fastidio, perche non si discerne.]

The intonation problems would arise primarily in simultaneous realizations on fretted instruments in conjunction with fixed pitch keyboard instruments. Doni's solution, to ornament the bass part, will be discussed below; it may apply mainly to dramatic music, which is the subject of Doni's discussion.

There are, however, other ways of overcoming the intonation problems than by using diminutions. By playing only the bass line itself, the performer can adjust the intonation of individual notes as needed, a procedure perfectly feasible for an accomplished performer on a fretted instrument. The open strings are tuned to the keyboard instrument and present no intonation problems. The important point of Doni's remark is that when the extended lutes are used with keyboard instruments, simultaneous realizations are musically undesirable and seem not to have been used.

Contemporary evidence suggests a wide acceptance, at times even a preference, for having the the extended lutes play the bass part. Praetorius (1619b, 2:52) speaks favorably of the use of the theorbo as a bass-line instrument: "The theorbo sounds quite lovely when it . . . plays together with bass instruments or in their stead [Die Theorba ist auch gar lieblich anzuhören wenn sie . . . nebenst dem Bass oder anstatt des Basses gebraucht wird]."

Coming at a time when the theorbo was extensively used to accompany monodies, Praetorius's statement is an early acknowledgement of its function as a bass instrument. Francesco Turini goes further than that and implies that the chitarrone is preferable to any other instrument for playing the bass part in ensemble music that includes violins. The preface to his

Madrigali a cinque cioè tre voci e due violini, libro terzo reveals a great deal about the function of the extended lutes and is worth quoting in full:

> Although these madrigals can be concerted with a keyboard instrument alone without chitarrone; or with a chitarrone or other similar instrument without the keyboard; nevertheless, they make a much better effect together, since the keyboard instrument does not give that spirit to the violins that the chitarrone gives, and the chitarrone alone without the keyboard results in an accompaniment [which is] too empty in the middle parts, more so in the ligatures [long, sustained notes]; and dissonances, and much more so in the high [notes]; and [those high notes] at the lower octave does not give good results.
>
> In order to [reach] this effect, the basso continuo has been duplicated to serve not just the chitarrone, but also the *bassetto da braccio, viola da gamba*, bassoon, and other instruments [which] concert well with the violins, but do not succeed continuously as does the chitarrone.
>
> Be advised that [the chitarrone] should play only when the violins play and when all the parts play and sing together, which can be easily be done by noticing the text placed above the bass line, which tells you when everyone [plays together], when [just] the violins, and otherwise. Also (in case there would be only a few of the above-mentioned instruments), the director can easily advise and replace the parts according to need with the same above-mentioned text, and also understand the nature of the composition, when the beat is spirited and when [it is] slow. (Mason 1983, 45–46)

> [Ancor che i presenti madrigali possino esser concertati con l'istromento solo da tasto senza chitarrone; overo un chitarrone, ò altro simile istromento senza quello da tasto; nulladimeno faranno assai miglior riuscita con l'uno, & con l'altro; poiche l'istromento da tasto no dà quel spirito a i violini che dà il chitarrone, & il chitarrone solo senza l'istromento da tasto riesce troppo vuoto ne li accompagnamenti de le parti di mezzo, & massime nelle ligature, & durezze, & molto più ne le alte; & sonar alla ottava bassa no fà buona riuscita.
>
> Onde à questo effetto si è fatto il presente basso continuo duplicato quale serve, non solo per il chitarrone, ma anco per un bassetto da Braccio, Viola da gamba, Fagotto, & altri si fatti istromenti, concertando tutti bene con i violini, mà non riuscendo simili sonati continuamente come fa il Chitarrone.
>
> Si avertira di sonarli solamente quando sonano i Violini, & quando sonano, & cantano tutte le parti insieme; il che facilmente si può mettere in essecutione, avertendo alle parole poste sopra questo Basso Continuo, cioè ove dice quando Tutti, & quando Violini, & simili oltre, che serve anco (in caso che non vi sia alcono de i sudetti istromenti) per che regge la battuta potendo facilmente per le medesime sudette parole avisare, & rimettere la parti secondo il bisogno, & conoscere benissimo la natura della Compositione quando vada battuta spiritosamente, & quando adagio. (Turini 1629, preface)]

Writing in 1629 Turini still uses the term chitarrone, but the manner of playing he describes is what above has been associated with a later time when the instrument is called theorbo. And we shall see that the use of the instrument on the bass part goes back even further to the very first years of the seventeenth century.

According to Turini the ideal performance of his pieces includes both harpsichord and chitarrone. The latter does not play continuously, however, but only with the violins and in the tutti passages. The list of single-line instruments that may substitute for the chitarrone suggests that this instrument played the bass part alone without a realization.

The pieces may be performed without harpsichord. The chitarrone part is unusual in containing the complete continuo line, suggesting perhaps that the instrument played continuously in the absence of a harpsichord. Even so the result was flawed because of emptiness in the middle. This emptiness may have come about by the chitarrone's playing only the bass line; Turini is not explicit on this point. A realization would not help much, however, since the chitarrone chords are in a rather low register because of the lowered tuning of the two top strings. In short, the chitarrone is not suitable for playing the continuo part alone, with or without attempting to make a realization.

Turini's reason for using the chitarrone is to give "spirit" to the violins. The harpsichord, although a plucked instrument like the chitarrone, is incapable of providing this effect. Other bass instruments such as the small bass violin, the gamba, or the bassoon may substitute for the chitarrone, yet, none of them is fully satisfactory. The chitarrone is uniquely suited to play the bass part in ensembles involving instruments because of the special boost they give to the violins, a boost that no other instrument is capable of giving.

The preference for the theorbo as a bass-line instrument may be part of the reason why the bass violin developed so much later than the violin. The theorbo provided a musically desirable effect in conjunction with violins, and it was only at a later time that the concern for a homogenous string sound came to guide the choice of bass instrument.

The chitarrone, at the beginning of the seventeenth century, was thought of as especially suitable for accompanying the human voice. It is therefore quite remarkable that the rationale for including this instrument in Turini's pieces is unrelated to the vocal aspect of his work, but instead has to do with the effect of the chitarrone on the two violins. And it seems beyond coincidence that the repertories in which the chitarrone is widely used all feature two violins: dance collections and chamber sonatas, church sonatas, and sacred concerted music.

The relationship between the harpsichord and the extended lutes in the early seventeenth century involves a curious paradox. In one context the two may be thought of as similar, while in another they are dissimilar. This distinction is not merely a matter of semantics but is important for the understanding of instrumental usage at that time.

Within the repertory of vocal monodies the harpsichord and the chitarrone may be thought of as similar instruments in that each one supplies a realization of the bass. When the accompaniment to a monody is specified as "chitarrone o altri simili istrumenti" (Dognazzi 1614) the implication is that a chordal instrument is needed. Indeed, a large number of published monodies mention both the harpsichord and the chitarrone because they are the preferred instruments of accompaniment.

In the title Turini calls for *chitarrone o simil instrumento*. "Similar" in this context must mean something other than a harpsichord which is already included. Within Turini's work the chitarrone and the harpsichord function as different kinds of instruments, one suitable for playing the bass line alone, the other for playing realizations. The division of labor is justified by Turini's preference for the chitarrone over other instruments to play the bass; it is also supported by Doni's observations on intonation problems in simultaneous realizations, cited above.

Turini's and Doni's observations together provide a convincing rationale for considering the extended lutes as single-line instruments, particularly when used together with violins or with keyboard instruments. Within certain contexts, then, the chitarrone is to be regarded as dissimilar to the harpsichord and similar to single-line bass instruments such as the bassetto da braccio, the viola da gamba, and the bassoon.

When early seventeenth-century titles call for "chitarrone or another similar instrument," this expression may refer to either a chordal instrument or a bass-line instrument. A problem arises in deciding on the proper choice, for instance in Salomone Rossi's third book of instrumental music for two violins and chitarrone, *o altro stromento simile* (1613). Traditionally this expression has of course been taken to refer to another chordal instrument. Stylistic considerations, however, favor performance of the bass without a realization (see chap. 7), and the use of the chitarrone points in the same direction. Like Turini, Rossi may well have chosen this instrument because of its ability to give spirit to the violins.

Rossi's first book of instrumental music (1607) calls for "chitarrone o altro istromento da corpo," which normally is taken to mean an instrument capable of producing a "body of sound," in other words, a realization. But, given that the chitarrone most likely played only the bass line, one should expect the substitute to do the same. It makes better sense to consider the "istromento da corpo" to be an instrument with a large body or belly: bass violin, bass gamba, lute, etc.

The extended lutes are frequently mentioned for the accompaniment of monodies up to about 1630. After that time these instruments are most often encountered in ensemble music which involves a keyboard instrument and/or violins. The repertory includes opera, church sonatas, concerted vocal music, and to some extent dance music and chamber sonatas, though here the extended lutes are relatively rarely mentioned. In short, it would appear that the principal function of the extended lutes in seventeenth-century music other than the early monody is that of a bass-line instrument. This inference is supported by the stylistic requirement of the music as well as by evidence found in the performing parts.

The most extensive seventeenth-century use of the extended lutes is in church music, in the *sonata da chiesa* and in concerted vocal music. The instrumental ensemble in the concerted repertory became standardized quite early in the century so as to consist of two violins and — sometimes but not always — bass (see chap. 6). The pieces in the canzona-church sonata tradition also became standardized so that after about 1640 the instrumental ensemble in each of these repertories normally consisted of two violins (with or without bass).

Many publications list a number of interchangeable bass instruments that may be used. The title of G. B. Fontana's *Sonate* (1641) mentions bassoon, chitarrone, cello, and then adds "or other similar instruments"; P. Cornetti's *Motetti concertati* (1638) specifies chitarrone, bassoon, or violone. Cavalli, in the preface to the *Musiche sacre* (1656), expresses his preference for the *violoncino*, but the printer adds that the bass also may be played by chitarrone, bassoon, or another similar instrument. It seems as if the choice of bass instrument was dictated, not by the preference of the composer, but by what kinds of instruments were available.

The bass instruments in sacred vocal music, like Turini's, participate only with the violins and in the tutti passages. But whereas Turini provides the complete continuo line in the chitarrone part, the composers of sacred music only include what is actually played. The bass part is not a doubling of the organ continuo but a separate orchestral part. There are no indications in this repertory for the chitarrone to play a realization, nor is there any more reason to do so than in Turini's work.

In canzonas and church sonatas the bass is a contrapuntal part similar in importance to the two violin parts. The organ continuo supplies the realization and the theorbo functions as a single-line bass instrument. A theorbo realization would obscure the contrapuntal qualities of the bass part and would therefore be quite inappropriate.

Wind instruments are rarely mentioned in publications of sacred music after 1650, which means that the bassoon and the trombone disappear. At the same time, the extended lutes are mentioned more frequently than before. The bass parts in most of M. Cazzati's concerted works (1653, 1660b, 1663, 1665, 1666) give the option of performance on violone or theorbo, and other composers of such music follow suit.

Prominent composers of church sonatas, such as A. Corelli (1681, 1689) regularly allow the bass part to be played on either the extended lute or the violone. As already noted, the archlute reappears at this time in the church sonatas of Corelli and other composers, its agility being especially suitable for the fast moving contrapuntal bass parts. The theorbo does not disappear, however, but is mentioned in concerted vocal music well into the eighteenth century (Silvani 1725).

Using the extended lutes to play the bass line alone goes back to the early part of the seventeenth century. In the early part of the century the theorbo was used for continuo accompaniment as well, but as that function disappeared around 1635, bass-line playing became the principal use for the extended lutes. The archlute was not very prominent until about 1680, after which time it was employed in pieces that require agility rather than power. The performance of the bass part alone remained one of the most important functions of the extended lutes until their demise sometime in the first half of the eighteenth century.

14

The Extended Lutes as
Double Bass Instruments

The extended lutes, as the name implies, differ mainly from the regular lutes in the addition of open strings in the bass. Agazzari (1607, 8) refers to the open strings as the outstanding feature of the theorbo. Piccinini (1623, 6) gives them credit for being one of the two main reasons why the lute was abandoned in favor of the extended lute. He calls the open strings "contrabassi" — double bass strings — but is quite vague about their use. Piccinini's intabulated solo pieces do not make much use of the contrabassi, and it would seem that their value must have been greater when the theorbo was used in some other context.

Turini speaks of the theorbo as giving spirit to the violins while playing alongside the harpsichord. Played on the stopped strings, however, the bass part could hardly match the rich sound of a harpsichord realization. Judicious use of the contrabassi would add volume and the distinct color needed to make the part stand out. Such a performance would make sense in terms of the statements cited above, but there is no supporting documentation in the early part of the century.

The only documented case in which the theorbo takes on a double bass function is in Cazzati's *Sonate a due, tre, quattro, e cinque*, opus 35 (1665). The work includes a part for theorbo which alternately may be played by the contrabasso (ex. 2.1). The theorbo appears to be first choice, and the appropriate substitute is an instrument that performs in the lower octave. The importance of this document is heightened by the fact that no other printed double bass parts are known in Italy at this particular time. Moreover, Cazzati is a major composer, and Bologna, where he was employed at St. Petronio, was a major center of church music, so even a single piece of documentation may have far-reaching implications. The one just cited opens up the possibility that substituting the theorbo for the double bass may represent a general practice.

Developments toward the end of the seventeenth century support the idea that the theorbo at times functioned as a double bass. The contrabasso described by Bismantova (1978,118), also called *violone grande*, has the same range as the normal violone, with the lowest string tuned to G'. The range is nearly identical to that of the theorbo, which goes to A' (and perhaps sometimes to G'). Most double bass parts could be played on any one of these three instruments, contrabasso, violone, or theorbo, though the latter may have problems with chromatic alterations. Such alterations are not very frequent in the late seventeenth century, and changes of key between pieces could to a large extent be accommodated by retuning the bass strings on the theorbo as needed. In short, the theorbo, the small double bass, and the violone all have the same range and on that score could substitute for each other.

The concerted vocal music in the last decades of the seventeenth century often used an expanded orchestra with parts for both cello and violone. The surviving violone parts at S. Petronio in Bologna often contain features normally associated with the double bass such as the simplification of florid motion and downward octave transposition. Significantly, the violone in such works is commonly interchangeable with the theorbo. As discussed above (chap. 9), this kind of part may well represent a stage in the transformation of the violone from a bass instrument to a double bass instrument. The extended lutes could fulfill either function.

Late seventeenth-century sacred vocal music employs the theorbo rather than the archlute, which is more frequently associated with the church sonata. The difference in usage may be related to differences in sound between the two instruments. Dalton Smith (1979, 444) points out that seventeenth-century archlutes with double courses have a mellow sound with no noticeable break from the fingered to the unfingered strings. This instrument is clearly suitable for the contrapuntal parts in church sonatas. On the theorbo the single open strings have a more penetrating sound than the fingered strings, and in the large concerted works the part would project better if played in the lower octave. The preference for the theorbo in sacred vocal music might be a result of its strength in the double bass register and may suggest that the instrument in fact functioned as a double bass.

15

Ornamentation on the Extended Lutes

While the extended lutes frequently played the bass line alone without a realization, the part may not always have been played exactly as notated. A number of early seventeenth-century sources speak of the ornamented playing of the lute, and the practice is traceable until about 1640. The nature of the lute, extended or not, is such that the sound is best kept alive by restriking the strings, playing arpeggios, or ornamenting the part. This may be behind the "ornamenting" function in the early part of the century and may also have been reflected in the use of the extended lutes in later times.

A. Agazzari (1607) distinguishes between two different functions of musical instruments. Some are used for the realization of the bass, and others for ornamentation above the given bass. The lutes can be used in both capacities. Players of the ornamenting instruments need to know counterpoint in order to compose "new parts above the bass and new and varied passages and counterpoints" ([1607] Kinkeldey 1910, 219). Agazzari's favorite ornamenting instrument is the lute, and he describes its function in flowery language:

> He who plays the lute . . . must use gentle strokes and repercussions, sometimes slow passages, sometimes rapid and repeated ones, sometimes something played on the bass strings, sometimes beautiful vyings and conceits, repeating and bringing out these figures at different pitches and in different places; he must, in short, so weave the voices together with long *gruppi, trilli*, and *accenti*, each in its turn, that he gives grace to the consort and enjoyment and delight to the listeners. (Strunk 1950, 428)

> [Onde chi suona leuto . . . devesi dunque, hora con botte, e ripercosse dolci; hor con passaggio largo, et hora stretto, e raddoppiate, poi con qualche sbordonata, con belle gare e perfidie, repetendo, a cavando le medesime fughe in diverse corde, e luoghi; in somma con lunghi gruppi, et trilli, et accenti a suo tempo, intreciare le voci, che dia vaghezza al conserto, e gusto, e diletto all'uditori. (Kinkeldey 1910, 219)]

These comments may well describe the use of the archlute as well as the regular lute. The theorbo is described by Agazzari [1607] in somewhat more conservative terms:

The theorbo, then, with its full and sweet consonances, greatly supports the melody, lightly restriking and playing *passaggi* on the open strings (the outstanding feature of that instrument) with *trilli* and subdued *accenti*. (Strunk 1950, 429)

[La Tiorba, poi, con le sue piene e dolci consonanze, accresce molto la melodia, ripercotendo, e passeggiando leggiadramente i suoi bordoni, particolar eccellenza di quello stromento, con trilli, et accenti muti. ([1607] Kinkeldey 1910, 219)]

Agazzari mentions a number of different ornamenting instruments but only the extended lutes seem to have continued this function beyond the first decades of the seventeenth century. Doni (ca. 1635, 1:111), cited above, points out that the extended lutes always ornament their part when playing with keyboard instruments. The faster motion covers up intonation difficulties which would be particularly noticeable in the case of simultaneous realizations. While Doni's argument is musically sound one may question whether the ornamented playing really had its origin in intonation difficulties; it would seem more likely to have grown from the practice described by Agazzari.

Doni's mention of ornamented playing was corroborated by the account of musical life in Rome by André Maugars who visited the city in 1639. He describes how "the archlute accompany the organ, with a thousand variations and an incredible swiftness of hand"([1640] MacClintock 1979, 120). In another passage he describes the context for this kind of performance :

As to the instrumental music, it was composed of an organ, a large clavecin, two or three violins, and two or three archlutes. At times a single violin sounded with the organ, and then another answered; another time all three played different parts together; and then all the instruments repeated together. Sometimes an archlute performed a thousand variations on ten or twelve notes, each note five or six measures long; then another played the same passage differently, I remember one violin played purely chromatically. ([1640] MacClintock 1979, 119-20)

The ornamented playing occurred within a work that involved violins and sometimes interplay between violin and archlute. While the violins may or may not have played diminutions, it was the archlute part that caught the listener's attention. The degree of ornamentation went considerably beyond adding diminutions to a bass line as described by Doni. At times the archlute would elaborate on notes sustained over several measures, perhaps a ground bass or a cantus firmus.

By way of summary, according to early seventeenth-century statements on the ornamented playing of the extended lutes, it appears that this practice had its roots in renaissance diminution practice. It is not a form of accompaniment, but an embellishment of the bass part. The ornamented playing was still being practiced in Rome in the late 1630s in sacred music and in dramatic music.

Bass lines in music at this time were not melodically interesting and must have benefitted a great deal from being ornamented. If or when such ornamentation was applied to arias, the bass must have taken on the character of an instrumental obbligato. The true obbligato aria came into existence around 1670 and it is rather suggestive that the obbligato is a bass part that was played on the cello. The accounts of Doni and Maugars suggest that the prominence now given to the bass conceivably may have developed from a tradition of ornamenting that part on the extended lutes.

Arias from the middle of the seventeenth century, whether in secular or in sacred music, very rarely employ instruments except for the continuo and occasionally a string orchestra. A nearly unique exception is an aria with theorbo from an anonymous oratorio (ex. 3.2). The work is found in a manuscript containing music by Marco Marazzoli (d. 1662) and Luigi Rossi (d. 1653) and belongs stylistically to the same period (I-Bc MS Q.45).

Though written a decade or two before the appearance of the first basso obbligato arias, the theorbo part in the example is in several respects similar to the bass in such arias. The instrument is active mostly in the ritornelli, playing diminutions on the slow moving bass. At the end of the aria is a section with motivic interplay between the voice and the theorbo, highly unusual in music from this time. The importance of this example lies in showing an exposed part for the theorbo in a repertory where single instruments never seem to be similarly featured. At the very least it suggests that the ornamenting role of the instrument was not totally forgotten.

Another aria that may reflect the practice of ornamented playing on the extended lutes is from Alessandro Scarlatti's opera *Le nozze col nemico* (I-Nc MS 33.3.17, fol. 87). The piece is marked *Aria di gusto Leuto* — "aria in the lute style." The element that links the aria to the lute is the bass ornamentation. The original version has only the embellished instrumental line. In example 3.3 the harmonically active notes have been extracted and added on a third staff; this new part approximates what a figured bass player might have played. The notation on three staves makes clear the way in which the aria was performed and its similarity to the oratorio aria above.

While these examples seem to be the only ones linking diminutions to the extended lutes, they are not alone in pointing toward florid playing of these instruments. Florid realizations, such as the arpeggiation described by Piccinini (1623, chap. 12) may to the listener have had an effect similar to what Maugars describes. Piccinini's comments are echoed a century later in a cello piece by Joseph M. C. dall'Abaco with the inscription *Arpeggiate a modo d'arciliuto* — "arpeggiated in the manner of the archlute." Neither of

Example 3.2.   Anonymous Aria with Obbligato Theorbo, ca. 1650

Example 3.3.   A. Scarlatti, Aria from *Le nozze col nemico*

these examples is specifically concerned with accompaniment, yet both suggest that arpeggiation is characteristic of the way the extended lutes are played.

The arpeggiated playing associated with the extended lutes may have a bearing on figured bass accompaniments on these instruments. In operas the archlute is sometimes specified for the accompaniment of arias in place of the harpsichord. In Alessandro Scarlatti's *Il prigioner fortunato* (GB-Lbl MS Add 16126) the instrument is mentioned a number of times for the accompaniment of sicilianos, an aria type much used by this composer.*

Having in mind the possibility that an arpeggiated realization might be in order, one may note with interest that J. S. Bach chose precisely that kind of accompaniment in two instrumental sicilianos. Both pieces occur in works with obbligato harpsichord, namely, the flute sonata in E flat (BWV 1031) and the violin sonata in C minor (BWV 1017). While the violin siciliano employs the same patterned arpeggiation throughout, the flute siciliano (ex. 3.4) has somewhat more elaborate figuration with occasional nonharmonic tones. In his obbligato sonatas, as in his music in general, Bach prefers contrapuntal interplay between the principal parts rather than melody and arpeggiated accompaniment. The use of such accompaniment in two sicilianos, seen in light of Scarlatti's use of the archlute in similar pieces, is at the very least suggestive. Bach may have been imitating a well-known idiom, thereby providing a distant reflection of archlute accompaniment in Italy.

The substitution of arpeggios for block chords in the accompaniment considerably alters the character of any composition. Sicilianos are usually played with chords on the first and third beats of every group of three. That requires a tempo sufficiently fast to keep the pattern rhythmically alive and yet provide a slow, lilting feeling. Because Bach used sixteenth-note motion, the element of continuity is already there; rather than a lilt, there is a sense of smooth flow. The tempo can therefore be taken slower than would have been the case with a chordal realization and a bass moving in quarter and eighth notes. The result is greater emphasis on melodic qualities and less on rhythm, something that would seem most appropriate in a slow operatic aria from around 1700.

---

* MS Add. 16126 in the British Library, Scarlatti's *Il prigioner for-tunato*, contains unusually detailed markings of instrumentation, while in the Naples MS the markings are sparse (Conservatorio di Musica San Pietro a Maiella MS 31.3.32). When the London MS calls for "Violoncello, e leuto" the Naples version sometimes only mentions the cello. This suggests that when the cello is mentioned in other scores, a not uncommmon occurrence, the intention may be to include the (arch-) lute as well.

Example 3.4. J. S. Bach, *Siciliano* from Sonata for Flute and Obbligato Harpsichord, BWV 1031

The difference between the chordal accompaniment and Bach's florid line is substantial, and that would be the case with any piece given a similar treatment. The possibility that the extended lutes functioned as ornamenting instruments in music from the middle of the seventeenth century suggests that the tempo and character of many pieces may have differed a great deal from the impression given by the surviving continuo parts.

16

Conclusion to Part Three

The popularity of the extended lutes during the baroque period is quite understandable in light of their versatility. Traditionally considered to be chordal instruments, they did indeed handle continuo parts. The theorbo was widely used for the accompaniment of secular monodies at the beginning of the century. The role of the extended lutes as continuo instruments has, however, been exaggerated, and after 1635 this function appears to have been of secondary importance.

The most common use of the extended lutes was on the bass line, sometimes playing the bass as notated, frequently featuring the open strings so that the effect would be akin to that of a double bass. The theorbo is particularly prominent as a bass-line instrument and is employed in all genres of ensemble music.

The archlute was generally less used than the theorbo. It may have carried on the tradition of the ornamenting instruments described early in the seventeenth century and in doing so influenced the development of the basso obbligato aria. However, due to the employment of wound strings in the latter part of the seventeenth century, the archlute became the most versatile instrument among the extended lutes. It could handle treble obbligato parts in arias, bass and double bass parts, and continuo accompaniment. It was widely used in opera and oratorio, and also in church sonatas.

Early in the eighteenth century the extended lutes fell victim to the increased demands for volume and the refinement and specialization of instruments with a single function. The cello and double bass were superior to the extended lute in their respective capacities, and treble obbligato parts were better projected by wind or string instruments. Continuo playing, never an easy task on the extended lutes, was more efficiently done on keyboard instruments.

When the *maestro di capella* at San Marco in 1714 tried to hire players of extended lutes he could not find qualified applicants (Arnold 1966, 6). Benedetto Marcello, also a Venetian, in his satirical *Il teatro alla moda* (ca.1723) fails to mention the extended lutes at all. Everyone, from the prima donna to the double bass player, is the subject of unkind comments, and the archlute would have been a grateful object of satire. The omission suggests that the instrument no longer played a prominent part in opera. Though extended lutes remained in use for some time, they had essentially outlived their usefulness by the time Marcello was writing.

Part Four

The Realization of the Continuo Bass

17

The Early Seventeenth Century

The central issue in continuo practice, the preceding discussion notwithstanding, is the realization of the bass. A great deal has been written about the subject, and there is no need to recapitulate ideas easily available in the standard literature. The focus here is to discuss and evaluate the source material, including a number of items that have not previously attracted attention.

Most of the new source material comes from the early eighteenth century. A number of solo cantatas from that time have written-out harpsichord parts, as do some other works. One needs to establish whether these parts may be taken as models for realizations, or whether they are exceptional cases in which the composer had specific ideas about the accompaniment that could not be expressed by writing out the bass part alone.

Another set of sources, of perhaps greater importance, is the group of figured bass methods by Neapolitan composers, known as *partimenti*. These methods have for a long time been considered outside the mainstream of Italian continuo practice, but that view needs to be revised. This material, never before scrutinized, adds a new perspective to eighteenth-century thoroughbass developments.

A third source that needs at least some attention is a treatise in the Marciana library in Venice entitled *Precetti ragionati* (I-Vnm, MS 10269). This bogus manuscript, dated 1664, has never been discussed in the musicological literature, and it is high time for its spurious nature to be documented.

The birth of the basso continuo practice has been extensively documented in studies by Kinkeldey (1910), Schneider (1918), and Arnold (1931); Arnold prints large portions of the original documents in translation. Though written in the form of an instructional method, *Figured Bass Accompaniment* by Peter Williams (1970) contains many illuminating insights; his is also the only study to distinguish among the various national styles of continuo realizations. Many aspects of the early development of the basso continuo were discussed above in conjunction with matters concerning the origins of the practice (chap. 2); these will be touched upon only briefly in the following pages.

The Sources

When the first continuo parts appeared (Croce 1594, Banchieri 1595) the composers included no instructions for making a realization. Evidently the practice had been in existence for some time and was considered common knowledge. During the first decade of the seventeenth century information about continuo realizations appears in a number of different kinds of sources. Prefaces, such as the one to L. Viadana's *Cento concerti* (1602) often provide valuable insights. Larger works on musical practice, such as Banchieri's *L'organo suonarino* (1611), may touch on continuo practice.

Two primary sources of special importance are Agazzari's *Del sonare sopra il basso con tutti stromenti* and Bianciardi's *Breve regola per imparar' a sonare sopra il basso*, both published in Siena in 1607. Bianciardi is exclusively concerned with the realization of the bass, while Agazzari deals more broadly with the subject, suggesting that certain instruments engaged in elaborate improvisation. Each work contains brief examples of realizations that illustrate and clarify the general principles for accompaniment. Other examples of this kind are found in tablatures for the extended lutes (Kapsberger, 1610; Castaldi, 1622).

The Context

Appearing in a time of transition, these early sources on the basso continuo reflect practices of the past while at the same time establishing the foundations for the practice of the future. Three different traditions are discernible. Least important is diminution practice, which is mentioned only by Agazzari. More important are the two traditions of accompanying vocal polyphony, either by duplicating all the parts, or by playing a realization of the bass.

The duplication of the voice parts on the organ is a cumbersome way of accompanying that essentially had been abandoned by 1620 (Horsley 1977). Agazzari points out that many organists were ill prepared to play from scores, and in doing so would accumulate an excessively large library ([1607] Kinkeldey 1910, 221). Viadana (Arnold 1931, 20) pays lip service to the use of scores but includes only the continuo bass in his publications.

One of the puzzling aspects of early continuo practice is Agazzari's ([1607] Kinkeldey 1910, 216, 219) division of continuo instruments into two classes, instruments of foundation, which perform the bass as notated, and instruments of ornamentation, which "invent new parts above the bass, and new and varied passages and counterpoints." Among these are the lute, theorbo, harp, *lirone*, cithern, spinet, violin, pandora—in other words, mostly plucked instruments. Agazzari's description of the ornamenting instruments has been the subject of extensive commentary and, to some extent, conflicting interpretations (Goldschmidt 1895, Rose 1965, Brown 1981).

Agazzari's treatise is appended to a collection of sacred music, the field in which the composer was most active. There are other descriptions of performances at this time in which large numbers of instruments and voices are mixed (Banchieri 1609a, 49–50), and in such cases the ornamented playing seems appropriate. However, a few decades into the seventeenth century the concerted works tend toward a standard instrumentation with written-out parts for two violins and, sometimes, bass instrument, as in Gallerano's *Messa e salmi* (1629). The free mixing of voices and instruments is a sixteenth-century tradition, associated with the multi-part repertory of that period, and therefore not suitable for the monodic style.

A vestige of the ornamented playing survived in the performance of members of the lute family. Agazzari singles out the lute as the principal instrument of ornamentation ([1607] Kinkeldey 1910, 219); he may well have meant the archlute, because at this time there was little difference between the two. The playing of the archlute is described by Doni (ca. 1635, 1: 111) and Maugars (MacClintock 1979, 119) in terms suggestive of ornamented renditions (see chap. 15). This kind of performance may have had a more narrow application than indicated by Agazzari, but continued well into the seventeenth century. However, ornamented playing seems to be applicable to continuo realizations only in pieces that include a separate part for the archlute.

The playing of an accompaniment from full score and the use of instruments of ornamentation are transitional phenomena in the early seventeenth century. Neither activity is very important after 1600, and the core of the emerging continuo practice is the accompaniment from a bass part. That is a practical multipurpose solution to the problem of constructing an accompaniment, equally suitable for the new monody and for large-scale concerted works for the church. It is relatively easy to learn, particularly when compared with playing from a full score. This point is emphasized in many of the early sources and is at the heart of the longevity of the continuo practice.

In abandoning the exact duplication of the parts in the accompaniment of vocal ensemble music, the continuo is reduced to a neutral chordal background against which the contrapuntal lines stand out. The continuo is not to be perceived as a separate part with its own musical integrity, but as support for the principal parts. The same is true in the monodic repertory.

The words and the vocal line are central, and the accompaniment is clearly subordinate. When Viadana says that the organist must play the organ part in a simple manner ([1602] Arnold 1931, 20) he more or less states the obvious. The written-out realizations by Agazzari and Bianciardi (ex. 4.1) and the intabulated accompaniment to monodies amply illustrate the point (Buetens 1973).

The task of the accompanist, then, is a fairly simple one, namely, to provide the correct harmonies in an unobtrusive manner. Specifically, the player must be able to see the chordal implications in a figured or an unfigured bass, in order to dress the harmonies in a texture suitable for the character of the music with voice leading that is not aurally objectionable.

Finding the Right Chord

The best way to guide the continuo player to the right chords is to figure the part adequately. This simple solution was, however, only partially adopted. Of the numerous collections of secular songs published between 1602 and 1635 less than half contain figures (Joyce 1981, 75). A century later the situation is not much changed, as can be seen in the works of Vivaldi (Kolneder 1970, 75). When present, the figuring is often incomplete and in need of additions and/or emendations. The accompanist must be prepared to play from an unfigured bass as well as from one with figures, and manuals and treatises regularly address both situations.

The chordal vocabulary in the early seventeenth century is limited, at least compared to that of the eighteenth century, and relatively few figures are needed. First inversion chords and dissonances call for Arabic numbers, and chromatic alterations for accidentals. Some composers in the early years use composite intervals indicated by the numbers 10, 11, 12, and even larger. This attempt to control the texture probably grows from concerns similar to those of organists who played from scores. Such control goes against the basic premise of continuo playing. Voice leading and choice of texture is the responsibility of the accompanist and not of the composer. Composite figures never gained much popularity and disappeared within a short time.

Bianciardi is particularly concerned about the realization of an unfigured bass. He gives elaborate rules, taking as the clue the motion of the bass part. Some of his rules have wide application; for example, when the bass moves a half step, the first chord takes a sixth. More often the rules have limited application, and most of them have exceptions. They may be helpful for the beginning accompanist who needs a frame of reference, but they are not reliable guides for dealing with unfigured bass lines.

Example 4.1.   Continuo Realizations Notated by A. Agazzari and F. Bianciardi

Agazzari

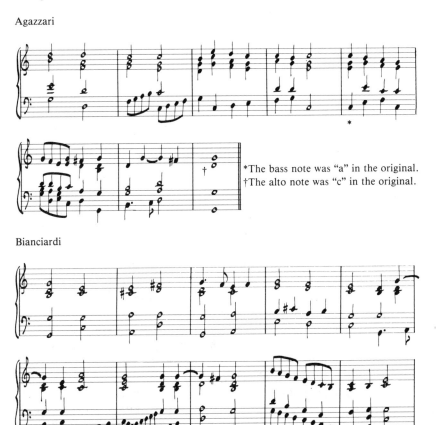

*The bass note was "a" in the original.
†The alto note was "c" in the original.

Bianciardi

Agazzari ([1607] Kinkeldey 1910, 217) does not even attempt to formu-late rules for unfigured basses. He holds that the harmony in vocal music is governed by the meaning of the words and that the progressions are unpre-dictable. Consequently, the player must rely on the ear. This advice is echoed in comments by numerous musicians at the time such as Fergusio (1612), Porta (1620), Brunetti (1625), and Cavaliere (1634, 35). Agazzari's advice about relying on the ear is the best guide not only for continuo players at the time, but today as well.

Realizations: Specific Recommendations

The early writers on continuo realizations are not much concerned with details but tend to offer broad recommendations based on general principles. Many of these are derived from counterpoint. The recommendations are positive in nature, telling the accompanist what to do rather than what to avoid. Most of the advice deals with texture and voice leading, with a few other matters added.

Texture

The texture of the accompaniment needs to be adjusted according to the size of the ensemble. With a full choir Agazzari recommends full sonorites, while with a small group one should reduce the number of parts ([1607] Kinkeldey 1910, 218). Puliaschi (1618) wants his vocal solos to be accompanied with some variety, alternating between full and sparse textures according to the meaning of the words. Bianciardi says that the words may require full textures, and in exclamations one may even use extreme registers ([1607] Haas 1929, 52). All these comments must be understood in relation to a normal texture of three to four parts; a full texture probably means full chords in both hands. Depending on the demands of the text the accompaniment may change rapidly between full and thin textures.

A special way of enriching the texture is the addition of octaves in the bass. This is mentioned by Agazzari as one way of creating variety even with a sparse texture ([1607] Kinkeldey 1910, 218). Bianciardi points out that three voices often produce an inadequate sonority and that it is useful to add the lower octave ([1607] Haas 1929, 51). The doubling of the bass part is a particularly effective way of enriching the sonority since it adds more body to the sound than the addition of a single part in a higher register.

Agazzari ([1607] Kinkeldey 1910, 218) holds that the range of the accompaniment should be narrow and the register low in order to avoid interference with the soprano part. If his written-out realization (ex. 4.1) is to be taken as a guide, however, he really means the middle register. That is also the view of Cima (1610). Bianciardi ([1607] Haas 1929, 52) points out that variations in register may support the meaning of the text, the low register being suitable for mournful music, and the higher register for more cheerful moods.

Voice Leading

The basic principles of voice leading are the same as in counterpoint. Both Bianciardi and Agazzari emphasize contrary motion and point out that with leaps in one part the others should move by step ([1607] Haas 1929, 52; [1607] Kinkeldey 1910, 218). But Bianciardi breaks his own rule in his written-out realization (ex. 4.1) with a passage in which the outer parts move in parallel tenths.

Viadana points out that the organist is under no obligation to avoid parallel fifths or octaves ([1602] Arnold 1931, 21). Later generations modified this stance so that parallels between the outer voices were avoided. At the time, however, Viadana's view may well have had some currency because the realization by Bianciardi contains direct parallels in bar 10 and barely disguised parallels in bar 9.

Agazzari's often quoted injunction against doubling the soprano part aims at not obscuring the beauty of the solo ([1607] Kinkeldey 1910, 218). This recommendation certainly does not apply to choral music, which often was performed from score so that the soprano was duplicated throughout. Many of the short scores in the early part of the century include only the bass and the soprano. The preface to one such work, Girolamo Giaccobi's *Salmi concertati* (1609) states that the soprano part does not need to be played *all* the time, implying that it was played at least intermittently. Giaccobi suggests that the occasional doubling of the soprano part is needed to support the singer. One of Agazzari's concerns was to avoid confusing the soloist with diminutions of the top part, a sentiment echoed by Severo Bonini (1615).

Agazzari assumes that the continuo player understands the need for proper resolution of dissonances ([1607] Kinkeldey 1910, 218), saying that the one who does not know will need to learn, presumably by studying counterpoint. In that case the student would also find out how to make a proper cadence by using a suspension. The early continuo instructions fail to discuss this subject but cadential suspensions are incorporated into the written-out examples by Agazzari and Bianciardi. The implication seems to be that the accompanist would provide proper cadences in the accompaniment whether indicated or not.

The last chord of a cadence normally takes a major third, but not always. Agazzari contradicts himself by first implying that a major third in a cadence is necessary, and then calling its occurrence "mostly true" ([1607] Kinkeldey 1910, 218).

Other Matters

Diminutions. While the realizations generally need to be simple a modest amount of ornamentation may at times have been acceptable. Viadana speaks of embellishing the cadences, and of adding some *passaggio* ([1602] Arnold 1931, 20). Giaccobi (1609) and Agazzari ([1607] Kinkeldey 1910, 218) also speak in terms of *passaggi*, and the intention seems to be that the accompanist may add florid motion of the kind associated with the diminution practice. All the writers are cautious on this point and the realizations are not likely to have been very elaborate.

Fast motion in the bass. Fast notes moving stepwise are thought of as a form of diminution so that only every second, fourth, or eighth note takes a chord. The realizations of Bianciardi and Agazzari (ex. 4.1) illustrate several different situations in which the performer has to decide how often to play chords. When the moving part includes skips of a fourth or more, each note in the bass receives a chord in both examples.

Fugal entries. Viadana explains how the organist duplicates the first entry in fugues and then is at liberty to play as he pleases ([1602] Arnold 1931, 20). In accompanying from a full score the player would of course have duplicated all the parts as they entered and that became a convention valid for the entire baroque era. Such a set of entries, notated in the continuo part in the clefs of the voice parts, at a later time became known as *bassetti*.

Continuo Solos

The history of sacred music up to 1600 is intimately intertwined with that of the cantus firmus principle. At the end of this period singers still improvised above a chant placed in the lowest part. When an instrumental practice of playing accompaniments from a bass part came into existence the two practices almost inevitably had to merge, the more so since both were central in the performance of sacred music. What emerged was a solo piece for organ written as a single line of music in the bass register; such pieces will be referred to by the expression "continuo solo."

The continuo solo was a direct outgrowth of the alternatim practice, in which the the organist was required to alternate with the choir in music ranging from hymns to masses. In the hymns the organist had to answer the choir with short verses, called versets, and it is in this genre that the continuo solo is born.

The first and only seventeenth-century publication that deals with continuo solos is Banchieri's *L'organo suonarino*, first published in 1605 and considerably expanded in the second edition (1611). The work includes a large number of "organ basses," short sections of music in bass clef which are often thought to be continuo accompaniments for unspecified pieces. Banchieri is not explicit on the purpose of these organ basses in the text. However, in the preface to the *Ecclesiastiche sinfonie* (1607), he mentions that the *L'organo suonarino* specifically addresses the question of how to use a basso continuo in the alternatim practice. In his study of the seventeenth-century organ hymn W. B. Keller (1958, 269–70) argues persuasively that Banchieri's organ basses could not have been used for the accompaniment of vocal compositions but must be organ versets written down in the form of a continuo line.

L'organo suonarino was reprinted in 1611 and 1622, and then posthumously in 1638, suggesting that the solo continuo versets were widely used. After Banchieri, however, the genre is not traceable until the early eighteenth century, then also in organ versets. The similarities to Banchieri's approach suggests that there must have been some kind of historical connection, and that the continuo solos led an underground existence until they again surfaced nearly one hundred years after Banchieri's publication.

The continuo solo reappeared in the works of the most important keyboard composer of his days, Bernardo Pasquini (1637–1710). His continuo solos are found in three manuscripts dated 1704–5 (GB-Lbl MS Add. 31501/I, II, III). One of the volumes contains *102 Versetti in basso continuo per rispondere al coro*; another contains an additional 108 versets. The pieces are all short, some only three measures long. Most of the versets are listed in groups with from three to ten pieces. While many consist of only a bass part, some of them have suggestions of voice leading in the other parts as well.

Pasquini recognized that the continuo solo had potential much beyond the simplicity of the versets and went on to write 28 multimovement sonatas for harpsichord, half of them for two instruments (GB-Lbl MS Add. 3105/I). Those for two instruments are mostly in three movements; the works for one instrument have from two to five movements.

Although some dance music is included, the sonatas are distinctly reminiscent of the *sonata da chiesa* in style and form. This is hardly a matter of coincidence. The origin of the continuo solo lies in the verset, and when Pasquini wanted to write large-scale works it is not surprising that he turned to a model associated with the liturgy, namely the church sonata.

The sonatas for one instrument mostly consist of a single line with a few passages in two parts. Example 4.2 shows a fugal composition. The countersubject is written out in the second measure and is probably to be included with the subsequent subject entries in bars 3 and 4, and later on as

Example 4.2.   B. Pasquini, Sonata, Continuo Solo

well. The number of entries suggests that the piece should be thought of as a four-part fugue, but there are no further clues to the realization.

The continuo solo became quite important in Naples at the beginning of the eighteenth century. The Neapolitan approach, discussed below, may well have a bearing on the realization of continuo solos by Pasquini.

18

Sources and Approaches after 1650

Manuscript Sources

While the emergence of the basso continuo in Italy has been studied extensively, its development throughout the remainder of the baroque era has
received very little attention. Some of the important sources have never
been subject to systematic study, let alone an assessment of their importance. Such an assessment must necessarily precede any attempt to develop
a broad perspective on the development of Italian continuo practice.

The flood of publications that comment on continuo playing in the
early seventeenth century is followed by a long drought, and even in the
eighteenth century there are relatively few important printed sources on the
subject in Italy. Manuscript sources are the principal guides to the practice.
Most of these would not have survived had it not been for the antiquarian
interests of Padre Martini. His well-known collection, today housed in the
library at the Music Conservatory in Bologna, contains a substantial number of works devoted to instructions in continuo playing. Most of these are
primers that add little to the understanding of thoroughbass practice. The
same can be said about similar works by well-known composers, such as A.
Scarlatti's *Regole per principianti* (GB-Lbl, MS Add. 14244) and B. Pasquini's *Regole* (I-Bc MS D.138).

With some danger of oversimplification, the manuscript sources on
continuo playing may be divided into two groups, though with a considerable amount of overlap. One group is characterized by taking a purely practical approach to the subject, dealing narrowly with the problems of realizing
the bass. The other group features a more comprehensive approach, in
which counterpoint and other subjects enter into the picture. Common to
both kinds of sources is the explanation of intervals and the use of figures,
and the description of chords as stacked intervals.

The central concern in all these works is the realization of an unfigured
bass. In that respect they are spiritual descendants of Bianciardi. Like him,
most of the writers base their rules on the motion of the bass part. Given a

certain interval between two bass notes the rule predicts the chords that will be used, particularly the second one. The problem and its solution is explained in the text, at times accompanied by an example. In these examples only the bass is written down and the solution is indicated by figures. Fully written-out examples are rare.

The approach changes somewhat in many sources from around 1700 and later. The realization of an unfigured bass is still important, but other subjects are added. Specific chordal progressions are shown, for example chains of seventh chords and cadential progressions. Some of these later works include exercises, a clear departure from the continuo instructions of the past.

The comprehensive approach to continuo playing can be traced back to Banchieri's *Dialogo musicale*, found in the second edition of *L'organo suonarino* (1611, 57–65). Banchieri summarizes the ideas of Viadana, Bianciardi, and Agazzari, and adds his own view on how to learn continuo playing.

The first step in Banchieri's approach consists in learning to sing (and simultaneously play) various scales written in bass clef using solmization syllables. The next step is to add more parts so that the realization at first is in two parts, then in three parts, and finally in four parts. In the examples each part is written on a separate staff together with Arabic numbers indicating the interval from the bass.

Banchieri's approach is distinctly contrapuntal, emphasizing the musical lines rather than chords. The method is quite impractical and had no emulators. However, the idea that many aspects of continuo playing ultimately have their roots in counterpoint is persuasive and is acknowledged by writers taking a purely practical view such as Agazzari. He takes for granted that the student understands basic voice leading in the resolution of dissonances, a matter pertaining to counterpoint, and says that the one who does not know will have to learn ([1607] Kinkeldey 1910, 218).

Banchieri's broadly conceived approach is reflected in a number of later sources. The titles often display concerns similar to those of Banchieri, as in the case of the 1663 manuscript *Regola di canto figurato, e contrappunto, et ancora il vero modo di suonare sopra la parte* (I-Bc MS P.138).

Another manuscript, also in Bologna, has an almost identical title: *Regole di canto figurato, contrappunto, d'accompagnare* (I-Bc MS E.25). This elaborate work of more than 200 pages is identical to another early eighteenth-century source, the *Regole per accompagnar sopra la parte* (I-Rc MS RI) well known for its discussion of full-voiced accompaniments and the inclusion of an aria with a fully written-out realization (Landshoff 1918).

The *Regole . . . d'accompagnare*, in accordance with Banchieri's recommendations, starts out with solmization exercises and then continues with explanations of basic notions such as intervals and types of melodic motion. A discussion of the natural progression of each interval forms the bulk of the work, and it is here that contrapuntal theory and continuo playing find a common ground.

Contrapuntal theory in the seventeenth century includes rules for the progression from one interval to the next, for example, how a sixth normally moves to an octave. If the bass is one of the parts, such a theory makes it possible to predict the progression from one chord to the next. In other words, the contrapuntal rules could serve as the basis for the realization of an unfigured bass. Agazzari ([1607] Kinkeldey 1910, 217) knew this argument and rejected it firmly, saying that the words determine the harmony so that no rules can be given for the realization of an unfigured bass. The author of the *Regole. . . d'accompagnare* was of a different mind, and his work is, in effect, a detailed spelling out of the harmonic implications of contrapuntal theory. That is why the majority of the musical examples are written out in five parts or more, and why the work, generally speaking, seems addressed to the continuo player rather than to the composer.

Learning accompaniment for the *Regole . . . d'accompagnare* is a laborious and involved undertaking, and one may question the extent to which it reflects actual practice. The question is of interest in assessing the importance of the written-out realization mentioned above, one of the few complete realizations of any continuo parts that survives from this time (ex. 4.3). The texture is very thick throughout the piece, having from six to ten parts. The harmony contains a liberal sprinkling of acciaccaturas (see chap. 21) and is one of the few sources to do so. The two hands frequently move in the same direction, and often one hand simply duplicates the notes of the other. Given the extremely theoretical orientation of the treatise and the crude texture of the realization one must question if the *Regole . . . d'accompagnare* should be used to exemplify any aspect of eighteenth-century continuo practice.

Printed Sources

Two widely known printed sources illustrate the changes that were taking place in continuo practice around 1700. Both works were reprinted a number of times and the views expressed must have been influential. L. Penna's *Li primi albori musicali per li principianti della musica figurata* was first published in 1672 and went through four editions, the last one from 1696. The book is a primer on music and deals with the three subjects found in the works discussed above: *canto figurato*, counterpoint, and figured bass. Though the title page refers to both organ and harpsichord the section on

Example 4.3.   Continuo Realization of an Aria, ca. 1710

thoroughbass mentions only the organ, and Penna's instructions are primarily for this instrument rather than the harpsichord. The content, as one might expect, centers on rules for realizing an unfigured bass.

Francesco Gasparini's *L'armonico pratico al cimbalo* was first published in 1708. It went through several minor revisions and a number of reprints up to 1802. This work marks a distinct departure from the past. By acknowledging the existence of major-minor tonality and modulations, Gasparini introduces a new dimension in the understanding of harmony that particularly affects his treatment of a bass without figures. The chapters on diminutions and recitative accompaniment give hints about the flavor of the realization totally absent in seventeenth-century sources.

The mention of the harpsichord in the title is indicative of the change in perspective this work exhibits. Aware of this, Gasparini included a note addressed to organ teachers, apologizing for the intrusion into their domain of teaching continuo accompaniment ([1708] 1963, 8). Gasparini's stated purpose is to ease the difficulties in the learning process, and to make continuo playing accessible for those who do not know counterpoint ([1708] 1963, 8, 10). His approach is guided by practical considerations — what is useful to the student. But the work is not designed for self study because at various points Gasparini addresses the teacher and suggests the kinds of exercises that may be assigned.

Much of the book is concerned with playing from an unfigured bass. In the introduction Gasparini speaks briefly of the problems with traditional rules which lend themselves to innumerable exceptions ([1708] 1963, 11), but declares that he will deal with them anyway. This is a bow to tradition, but in the end Gasparini makes a point of demonstrating the excessive complexity of this approach. Gasparini's own approach is based on an understanding of major and minor keys and the process of modulation — in other words, the basic ideas of the tonal system.

At the end of his discussion of tonality Gasparini provides a set of exercises that form the basis for the teaching of continuo playing in Italy for the rest of the century. The 21 exercises are identical except for being in different keys. Each one features a stepwise line ascending a sixth, then descending a ninth, and ending with a cadence (ex. 4.4). Each one has identical figures, illustrating the most common chords used in ascending and descending stepwise motion. By working through all the exercises the student would learn not only how to play in different keys, but also which chord is most likely to occur on each scale step.

Gasparini includes discussions of two subjects not encountered in the manuscript treatises: the accompaniment of recitatives, and the use of diminutions. The examples of recitative accompaniments illustrate the use of

Example 4.4.   F. Gasparini, Figured Bass Exercise

*These chords may have either a sharp 6 or natural 6.

full chords in both hands and the addition of acciaccaturas, i.e., unprepared dissonances not indicated by the figures.

The two chapters on diminutions are short, yet they suggest an accompaniment completely different from what was current in the seventeenth century. Used in an aria the diminutions would give the harpsichord part the character of an obbligato rather than an accompaniment. In short, Gasparini's treatise points to a radical break with the past in the manner of realizing the bass as well as in the method of teaching thoroughbass accompaniment.

The *Precetti ragionati* (1664): A Musicological Hoax

For someone willing to put together a fraudulent manuscript of some length, it seems odd to concentrate on music from the middle of the seventeenth century. Apart from Monteverdi the composers from this time are unknown, and so is the music. A fake manuscript on this period would hardly cause great damage, nor attract notoriety. Nevertheless, such a fake exists in the Marciana library in Venice under the title *Precetti ragionati per apprendere l'accompagnamento del basso sopra gli strumenti da tasto come il gravicembalo, il cembalo, etc.* (I-Vnm, MS 10269).

The treatise has the appearance of a genuine seventeenth-century manuscript: it is leather bound; the paper looks and feels old; the ink has occasionally soaked through and nearly obliterated the text on the opposite side. The musical calligraphy exhibits traits typical of the early seventeenth century: curved beams, and frequent use of triangular note heads. The title page gives the place and date of the manuscript: Venice 1664. In short, there is nothing in the appearance of the work that in any way suggests that the content is fraudulent.

The text of the book supports the impression of authenticity, containing frequent references to composers described as contemporary or recently deceased. Cavalli is said to be the most prominent living composer and many of his operas are mentioned, all of them written-well before 1664. The written-out examples of accompaniments include works by Monteverdi and Cesti, with realizations similar to those the author claims to have heard in performance. Compared to much seventeenth century writing on music, which often contains extensive references to antiquity and relatively infrequent references to contemporary practice, the *Precetti* is unusual in its focus on matters of interest to a twentieth-century reader.

The *Precetti* also contains ideas revolutionary for 1664. Confronted with the work for the first time, the reader is faced with an interesting question: how far to revise accepted views about the seventeenth century before starting to question the authenticity of the source. The church modes are completely abandoned in favor of major and melodic minor. That parallels the view of Gasparini (1708) and pushes the theoretical recognition of modern tonality back a generation or two. This is perhaps within the realm of possibility.

Keyboard players are told to practice scales in all 24 major and minor keys, using all five fingers more or less equally. The need to have command of all 24 keys is a corollary to understanding the principles of the tonal system. It would take an exceptionally perceptive musician to formulate this view in 1664, but it is perhaps not out of the question. The equal use of all five fingers of both hands is associated with the eighteenth century and seems unlikely at such an early time. So is the discussion of the fundamental bass (fol. 28ff), a concept originating with Rameau. Nevertheless, the unsuspecting reader may find it difficult to question the authority of what to all appearances is a genuine seventeenth-century treatise and instead consider the author way ahead of his time.

The full title of the *Precetti* is very similar to that of a well-known continuo manual from the late eighteenth century:*

Precetti ragionati per apprendere l'accompagnamento del basso sopra gli strumenti da tasto come il gravicembalo, il cembalo, etc.

Manfredini, Vincenzo. *Regole armoniche, o sieno precetti ragionati per apprendere i principij della musica, il portamento della mano, e l'accompagnamento del basso sopra gli strumenti da tasto, come l'organo, e il cembalo, etc.* Venice: Zerletti, 1775.

The similarities go much beyond the titles. Much of Manfredini's treatise is incorporated into the *Precetti*, filling folios 5–30 (out of a total of 47). Some of the material is rendered verbatim, more frequently there are changes. Manfredini's footnotes are often incorporated into the text. The musical examples are sometimes altered by substituting stepwise motion for broken chords (Manfredini 1775, 5; I-Vnm MS 10269, fol. 6v) and new

---

* I am indebted to Claude Palisca for pointing out the similarities between the titles of Manfredini's book and the *Precetti* which lead to the discovery of the relationship between the sources.

material may be added. The discussion of cadences (fol. 22r-27v) is based on Manfredini (53–55) but contains new examples by Frescobaldi, Praetorius, Merula, Monteverdi, and others (fol. 25v-27r). In short, most of the material in this section is taken from Manfredini but has been altered so as to justify 1664 as the date of writing.

Once identified as a hoax the *Precetti* is of little interest other than as a curiosity. The person who wrote it must have had extensive knowledge of seventeenth-century Italian music in general and of opera in particular. The Marciana library acquired the work in 1917 and at that time the number of people with such knowledge was quite small. It is hard to fathom the motives behind the involved labors that lead to the creation of the *Precetti*. It seems like a labor of love or of humor; certainly, the financial reward must have been miniscule.

19

Neapolitan Continuo Practice:
The *Partimenti*

The continuo solos of Pasquini were apparently not emulated in northern Italy. The genre did not succumb, however, but gained new life among Neapolitan composers under the name of *partimenti*. Composers such as Francesco Durante (1684-1755), Leonardo Leo (1694-1744), Carlo Cotumacci (1709-85), Fedele Fenaroli (1730-1818), and others wrote extended continuo solos of considerable complexity. The partimenti have been discussed and some have been published by Karl Gustav Fellerer (1930, 1938, 1940) but the genre has otherwise been ignored. One reason for the neglect is that the term *partimento* erroneously has become associated with continuo solos only, and that anything called by that name is considered outside of the thoroughbass tradition. As a result of the terminological confusion the *partimenti* are ignored by almost all writers on continuo practice, and the word is not even mentioned by Arnold (1931).

Partimento is one of many synonyms for basso continuo encountered in the early seventeenth century and it soon became the prevailing term in Naples (see chap. 2). The term, which remains in use all through the eighteenth century, may be defined as a bass note or a bass part that calls for a realization in the treble. That realization may be the accompaniment to a solo or an ensemble piece; it may also be an independent part so that the result is a keyboard solo. And since the Neapolitan teaching manuals on continuo playing contain only exercises — bass lines that need to be realized — these manuals are entitled *partimenti*.

The partimento manuals differ from most of the major sources on continuo practice in showing little if any concern for theoretical formulations and instead giving all the attention to practical concerns. While Gasparini, C. P. E. Bach, and their like mostly explain and illustrate what constitutes a good realization, the Neapolitans provide exercises to that end.

The systematic approach characteristic of these manuals seems to have been developed by Gaetano Greco (ca.1657-ca.1728). Though his teaching materials are imperfectly preserved (I-Nc, P.103) they illustrate the principal traits of the later manuals. The practical knowledge of keys is important, and Greco employs all 24, being perhaps one of the first to do so. Included in his teaching materials is a set of continuo solo versets, much like Pasquini's.

Greco's pedagogical ideas were developed and refined by Francesco Durante into a method that remained the model for Neapolitan teachers until the end of the century. Fenaroli's highly succesful partimento manual, reissued time and again and held in high esteem far into the nineteenth century, follows the format established by Durante. Durante's work, never published, remains the most comprehensive treatment of the subject, and also excels in terms of the musical quality of his excersises.

The full title of Durante's manual is *Partimenti, ossia intero studio di numerati. Per ben suonare il cembalo.** It falls into two large sections, the first concerned with the realization of the bass, the second with solo partimenti. While the exercises in the first part usually are preceded by a short, succinct statement about their purpose, the second part of the work contains no text whatever, nor any written-out examples. The interpretation of these textless sections is therefore at times quite problematical and any solutions must necessarily be hypothetical.

Durante starts out by having the student play standard progressions, cadential suspensions, and cadences in up to sixteen different keys. Then follow exercises that are central to the Neapolitan approach, which consists in harmonizing scales in ascending and descending motion. These scale exercises were later given the name *Regola dell'ottava*—"the rule of the octave" (ex. 4.5). The ideas behind this seemingly mindless repetition of a scale harmonization are the same as mentioned with Gasparini's exercises: to learn the most important inversions on each note of the chromatic scale, and to recognize the chord formation most likely to occur at a given scale step in major and minor keys.

While the octave harmonizations are helpful in dealing with an unfigured bass, Durante nevertheless includes exercises devoted to that subject. A great deal of attention is given to chains of 7th chords. The exercises contain progressions with different kinds of diminutions in the bass: eighth notes, sixteenth notes, and mixed motion.

The advanced exercises are divided into three sections. The first con-

---

* The three principal MSS for Durante's partimento manual are MS EE.171 at the Civico Museo Bibliografia Musicale in Bologna, MS M.14–7 at the Conservatorio di Musica G. Verdi in Milan, and MS M.S. 1869 at the Conservatorio di Musica San Pietro a Maiella in Naples.

Example 4.5.   F. Durante, Figured Bass Exercise: "Rule of the Octave"

Example 4.6.   F. Durante, Solo Partimento Exercise with Figures Showing
Motivic Interplay

tains 38 solo partimenti, the second contains about 50 diminution exercises, and the third contains 21 fugal partimenti. Most of the exercises fit on one page, but since the music is notated on only one staff-line, many of the pieces are of considerable length.

The opening section of the advanced exercises has no title. The first few numbers look like regular figured bass exercises, but that impression is soon dispelled. Some of the pieces contain passages written out in the treble clef, others are extensively figured so as to suggest melodic motion in the treble, and one piece has markings of solo and tutti.

In example 4.6 (I-Bc MS EE.171, fol. 14) the figures suggest a dialogue between the treble and the bass. The descending scale in the second measure may be imitated in the treble half a beat later, and an ascending scale may also be used at the beginning of the third measure.

Many of the exercises imply imitation by a change in the rhythmic activity of the bass. Typically, the bass initially presents a motif or a theme.

Example 4.7.   F. Durante, Solo Partimento Exercise with Imitation and Sequential
               Spin-Out of Subject

This is followed by slower motion which suggest activity in the upper part. Example 4.7 (I-Bc MS EE.171, fol. 16v) shows a somewhat elaborate version of such a case. A brief statement in the bass is imitated in the treble. Then follow sustained bass notes, which invite a sequential continuation in the treble based on the opening motif. The passage ends with a cadence, at which point the subject comes back.

Example 4.8 (I-Bc MS EE.171) starts with bass motion that suggests motivic interplay between the bass and the treble, followed by a passage written out in treble clef. The figures in the second and fourth measures indicate notes in the treble part; the number 8 has no meaning otherwise. The thin texture and the high register of the treble sections may suggest a solo effect that may be set in relief against a tutti effect created by using full chords and perhaps the more sonorous low register in the other sections.

The realizations suggested above, while hypothetical, have some basis in the notation. Other pieces, however, have no apparent clues, and the absence of any explanations by the composer makes it difficult if not impossible to recapture many of the features of solo partimento playing.

The second section of Durante's advanced exercises is in some documents identified as *partimenti diminuiti* (I-Nc MS Musica didattica 45–1–4). Each one starts with one or more written-out examples of florid motion above a simple bass progression. Then follows an exercise in which the bass progression is prominently featured in various keys and in modulating passages.

Example 4.9 (I-Bc MS EE.171, fol. 32) shows three different suggestions for diminutions, two in the treble and one in the bass. The basic progression, a half note moving up one half step, is later used in diminutions with four eighth notes substituting for the half note. The featured progression is not continually present; nevertheless, it seems that the realization should remain florid, or at least having melodic interest, all the

Example 4.8. F. Durante, Solo Partimento Exercise with Motivic Interplay and
Tutti-Solo Effect

time. The purpose of the exercises, in the end, is to enable the students to provide continuous diminutions given any kind of bass motion.

The third group of exercises consists of fugues. Most of the time only one part is given though two-part passages are not uncommon. The thematic entries in the exposition are usually notated in different clefs, just like the bassetti in continuo parts. Example 4.10 (I-Bc MS EE.171, fol. 61v) shows the fourth of Durante's fugal partimenti. It starts with three entries in descending order, in alto, tenor, and bass clefs, respectively. When the soprano enters, another part is temporarily added. The sequential passage starting in bar 7 suggests imitative interplay between bass and treble with the latter imitating the bass during the half note at the end of the measure and starting, as indicated, on the octave from the bass note.

The level of contrapuntal complexity expected in Durante's fugal partimenti is not likely to have been very high, and certainly nothing like what is found in Bach's keyboard fugues. Italian composers at this time are not remembered for their contrapuntal mastery, and the fugues of even as prominent a composer as Domenico Scarlatti are often little more than chordal progressions with a single moving part (for example the so-called Cat Fugue, K. 30). Durante's own pieces in this genre — some are found in

Example 4.9.   F. Durante, Diminution Exercise

primo modo   secondo modo   terzo modo

Example 4.10.   F. Durante, Fugal Partimento

his *Sei studii e sei divertimenti* — often feature parallel motion in thirds and sixths, chordal textures with one moving part, and prolonged sections in two parts. A realization of the fugal partimenti along these lines would not have been an insurmountable task for someone who has gone through Durante's advanced exercises.

Durante's teaching method is surely one of the significant documents in the history of continuo practice. Not only does it provide a solid grounding in fundamentals but it also helps develop specialized skills such as improvising a florid line above the bass. The diminution exercises are without parallels in the entire figured bass literature.

The advanced sections as a whole may be seen as a keyboard approach to learning composition. The player had to recognize at sight opportunities for using diminutions, imitations, motivic interplay, etc., and thereby developed compositional skills. A central aspect of this training was the necessity of working out musical ideas on the spot. The ability to compose quickly was particularly important in opera where a new work often needed to be completed in the course of a few weeks. The partimento method was uniquely suited to develop the facility needed for such a task. The method was developed and practiced at the Neapolitan conservatories, and it is hardly coincidence that their graduates dominated the field of opera for much of the eighteenth century.

20

Written-Out Keyboard Parts

One of the ideas behind the invention of the basso continuo is that the accompaniment is not important enough to warrant a fully written-out part, and that a shorthand version will suffice. Written-out keyboard parts are therefore rare, though not unknown. They range from brief suggestions of voice leading to fully written-out obbligato parts. These sources may seem like the most promising guides to the accompaniment as it was actually performed, but that is not always so. Each case needs to be evaluated to establish what it tells and what it does not tell about continuo accompaniment.

Most of the written-out parts occur in solo cantatas. In the second half of the seventeenth century it is not uncommon to find brief written-out passages in this repertory. The additions are usually written on the same staff as the continuo line but whether these passages should be played in such a low register is very much in doubt. Some sources speak of keeping to a low register, but the written-out examples early in the century suggest that "low" is a relative term (ex. 4.1).

These scattered examples mostly show details of voice leading and occasionally of imitations. Some manuscripts contain cases of similar voice leadings that point to the idiosyncrasies of a single performer or composer (Plank 1983, 11, 15). The modest amount of material added suggests that the accompaniment on the whole must have been very simple, as was the case at the beginning of the century.

A number of Stradella's cantata arias contain brief imitations written-out in two parts on the keyboard staff, but it is questionable whether these can be taken as models for realizations. Stradella was among the first, perhaps the very first, to write basso obbligato arias, and his occasional use of imitations is more likely a result of a general concern for making the continuo part interesting.

More extensive keyboard parts occur in cantatas from around 1700 and later. This trend seems to have started with Gasparini who, in his solo cantatas opus 1 (1695), includes three arias with instrumental obbligato

Example 4.11.   F. Gasparini, Aria from *Cantate de camera a voce sola,* Opus 1

parts that may be played on the harpsichord. Five years later the same publisher, Mascardi in Rome, brought out a similar collection by Bernardo Gaffi which contained six arias with written-out parts. Possibly under the influence of Gasparini, Benedetto Marcello and his brother Alessandro included a number of partially or completely written-out keyboard parts in their cantatas (Sites 1959).

In the preface to his opus 1 cantatas Gasparini says that some of the arias have two bass lines, of which one is for the convenience of the accompanist (see chap. 5). He also mentions that one of the parts may be notated in soprano or treble clef in which case the part is played with the right hand. Such passages occur mainly in sections where the voice rests; otherwise the part is notated in bass clef.

Example 4.11 shows one of these arias, *Il mio pianto sembra un gioco.* The piece is notated on three staves with the vocal part on top. The middle staff contains a florid bass part, and the lower staff, a simplified version of the florid part made for the convenience of the accompanist. It is a typical case of the continuo part having been constructed from the obbligato part by extracting the harmonically active notes.

In the preface Gasparini mentions that he has not fully been able to show his intentions, and that is all too evident to the reader. If the accompanist plays the lower line with the left hand, the right hand needs to play

Example 4.12.   B. Marcello, Aria from the Cantata *O gentil*

chords, and the florid line would have to be left out. If, on the other hand, the accompanist plays the florid line, it contains all the notes of the lower line. With a realization in the right hand this version would seem perfectly satisfactory, but it raises the question as to why the lower line is included at all.

Gasparini's unstated intention may have been similar to Gaffi's who, in his opus 1, included a number of arias similar to Gasparini's. In the preface the composer says that the extra line may be played by a violin or a violone (though adding that it is not really his intention to write cantatas with instruments and that the harpsichord alone may serve). The same provision would make sense in Gasparini's case. The aria in example 4.11 can be satisfactorily performed with keyboard alone, and only if another instrument plays the florid part does the accompanist need the simplified bass part.

The point of all this is that the florid part is not a written-out accompaniment but a basso obbligato. Gasparini's aria has a bass that earlier in this study (chap. 5) has been described as quasi ostinato. The opening bass pattern contrasts with the the vocal melody, and this contrast is maintained throughout the piece. The exact ostinato is abandoned, but the characteristic melodic and rhythmic figures are maintained. While at first glance Gasparini's aria, with its repeated figures, seems like a promising model for continuo accompaniment, a closer examination reveals that the piece tells us nothing at all about about that subject.

Benedetto Marcello, unlike Gasparini, wrote genuine keyboard parts which in certain respects may serve as models for the accompanist. Some of the parts consist in written-out ritornellos, such as in the aria in example 4.12 (I-Vnm MS 10752). At the beginning the harpsichord states the theme which is then immediately restated in the vocal part. Such dual statements of the opening theme were standard in arias at this time. However, the theme is normally presented in the bass part so that a cello or another bass instrument is needed to give the part the character of a solo. A harpsichord alone has difficulty doing justice to such a ritornello because the realization in the right hand obscures the melodic line in the left. Marcello wrote out

Example 4.13.   B. Marcello, Aria from the Cantata *O ch'io viva*

the opening solo in the treble register, thus making the participation of a cello superfluous.

Marcello's accompaniments implicitly acknowledge a problem in the performance of basso obbligato arias and also provide a solution. One may wonder if performers who were bothered by the same problem imposed a similar solution. In many arias the opening bass melody can easily be transferred to the treble and accompanied with the bass that later accompanies with the vocal statement of the same phrase. This solution has no documentary support but would in many instances make more musical sense than having the melodic part obscured by the realization.

In his quasi ostinato arias Marcello sometimes included idioms suitable for the harpsichord, such as in *Sotto del freddo* (ex. 4.13; I-Vnm MS 10752,

Example 4.14. B. Marcello, Aria from the Cantata *Sprezzata mi credei*

275). The incisive rhythm strikingly complements the sustained vocal line, and the low register and the sparse voicing provide an ideal accompaniment for an alto voice.

Another of Marcello's quasi ostinato arias, *La giu tra l'ombre* (I-Vnm MS 10752, 235) features idiomatic harpsichord arpeggiation (ex. 4.14). Like the preceding example this one also has a transparent texture.

The accompaniments in examples 4.13 and 4.14 are valuable as models in terms of texture and register. It is doubtful, however, that the keyboard figuration could be emulated in any other piece. In each case the keyboard patterns are embedded in the ostinato, so to speak, and the consistency of the figuration is only possible in an ostinato aria.

Written-out continuo realizations, as distinct from the composed keyboard parts of Marcello, are quite rare. Two surviving arias with written-out accompaniments show radically different approaches. The aria from the *Regole . . . d'accompagnare* (ex. 4.3), with a full-voiced realization, was discussed above and can hardly be considered as a model. Such a realization might be appropriate with a large ensemble in which the harpsichord needs to assert itself. But in an aria one would expect a certain amount of refinement, as in the case of Marcello's cantatas.

Not to be lightly dismissed is the realization in example 4.15, possibly by the composer, of an aria from Alessandro Scarlatti's cantata *Da sventura a sventura* (I-Nc MS 34.5.2). The texture is mostly in four parts. The voice

Example 4.15.   A. Scarlatti, Aria from the Cantata *Da sventura a sventura*

Example 4.16.   G. F. Handel, Sonata for Viola da Gamba and Obbligato Harpsichord,
Third Movement

leading is very carefully worked out, with a fair amount of passing motion
in eighth notes, particularly when the voice rests.

It is somewhat difficult to assess the importance of this realization
because of the rather sedate motion of the bass part. Scarlatti preferred the
obbligato bass, which usually gives rhythmic definition to the music. The
slowly moving bass in example 4.15 demands motion in the upper parts,
particularly when the voice rests, and that is rather the opposite of what
normally takes place. But this accompaniment is musically viable and, if
nothing else, says something about the range of possibilities at this time.

A sonata for viola da gamba and "cembalo concertato," attributed to
Handel (1858–94, 48:112–17), has a fully written-out harpsichord part. The
work is basically a *sonata da chiesa a due* in four movements. The principal
parts are the gamba line and the treble part of the harpsichord. Three of the
movements contain the usual imitative interplay between the principal parts
so that the harpsicord has an obbligato part rather than an accompaniment.

The third movement of Handel's sonata differs from the others in
having continual eighth-note arpeggiation in the harpsichord while the
gamba plays a slow melody consisting mostly of half notes or longer dura-
tions (ex. 4.16). The accompaniment features note values four times faster
than a standard realization, which would have one chord to each bass note.

The faster motion has a bearing on the tempo and therefore affects the character of the music. That, however, is consistent with Gasparini's examples of florid realizations (see under heading "Diminutions in the Accompaniment," chapter 21), where the treble tends to feature sixteenth notes while the bass has quarter notes. Like those examples, this little movement suggests that the accompaniment at times was considerably more elaborate than one might think from looking at the bass line.

21

Eighteenth-Century Continuo
Realizations: Selected Issues

Texture

The changes in accompaniment that took place in the late seventeenth century seem to have been directed at harpsichordists, but not at organists. Gasparini wrote from the point of view of the harpsichord performer, evidenced by the apologetic note to organists that prefaces his book. Durante's teaching method is, according to the title, specifically intended for the harpsichord. Organ accompaniments are rarely mentioned in the treatises and may have remained basically unaffected by the new tendencies.

A few writers commented upon what constitutes an appropriate texture on the organ. Bismantova says that the accompaniment should have no more than three or four parts (1978, 82). Gasparini echoes this comment, saying that pieces for one or two voices should be accompanied in four parts ([1708] 1963, 76). Gasparini also mentions that the organ may employ the "full style," meaning full chords in both hands, in works involving large performance forces.

The examples in part 4 of this book provide illustrations of a variety of harpsichord textures that may be used in accompaniments. The choice may have depended on the requirements of the piece, but also on the performance conditions, the size of the hall, the characteristics of the keyboard instrument, etc. The need for varied textures was expressed by writers at the beginning of the seventeenth century and is echoed at the end of the baroque period in the words of Pasquali (1757, 45–46). According to him, the accompaniment of vocal solos should always be transparent, and in tender places may consist of a single third or fifth. In more forceful passages the number of parts (Pasquali says chords) is increased, and octaves may be added in the bass. These recommendations are very similar to the advice offered by Agazzari in 1607.

Gasparini does not specifically address the problem of texture, though he mentions in one place that on the harpsichord "the filling or doubling of consonances as much as possible is not a thing to be avoided" ([1708] 1963, 76). The single-minded emphasis on full-voiced textures in the *Regole . . . d'accompagnare* (I-Bc MS E.25) is not musically convincing and the uniformly thick texture of the aria realization is hardly suitable to accompany a solo. Large ensembles, however, demand all the sonorous resources of the continuo instrument and full-voiced realizations are not only appropriate but necessary.

Voice Leading

The often heard injunction against doubling the notes of the solo part is not uniformly endorsed in the early seventeenth century, and eighteenth-century writers are also ambivalent. Gasparini strongly opposes such doubling, saying that one must never play the upper part note for note; rather, it suffices that the notes are contained in the harmony ([1708] 1963, 89). There is perhaps an implicit concern here that the singer have enough support to find the pitch, and an understanding that a proper realization will take care of that.

Other writers recommend more support for the vocalist. Bismantova ([1677] 1978, 82) prefers that the organist play all the notes of the solo part, or at least those on the main beats, in order to help the singer. Pasquali holds the same opinion, though pointing out that with instruments, such doubling of the principal part is undesirable ([1757] 1974, 45–46). Pasquali's comments suggest that the doubling of the vocal part may have grown from practical concerns such as helping the singer to find the pitch, or to stay in tune. Gasparini, writing from the perspective of one who works in the best opera houses at the time, is likely to have stated his view in purely artistic terms, and on those grounds Pasquali may well have agreed.

Recitative Accompaniment

The special problems of recitative accompaniment are treated by Gasparini ([1708] 1963, 78–84) and Pasquali ([1757] 1974, 47–48). Both authors recommend rich textures with full chords in both hands. Gasparini sometimes includes six or seven notes in one hand so that both the thumb and the little finger have to play two notes.

Gasparini says that the chords are played "almost like an arpeggio" ([1708] 1963, 79); he evidently means an unmeasured fast breaking of the chord. He specifically warns against continuous arpeggios or the use of ascending or descending scale passages, which would disturb the singer.

Pasquali is more explicit in his description of arpeggios, suggesting how the accompaniment may be adjusted to reflect the meaning of the text:

> Care must be taken not to strike [the chords] abruptly, but in the harpeggio way, laying down the fingers in the chords harp-like, *i.e.* one after another, sometimes slow, other times quick, according as the words express either common, tender, or passionate matters:
>
> For example; for common speech a quick harpeggio; for the tender a slow one; and, for any thing of passion, where anger, surprise, &c. is expressed, little or no harpeggio, but rather dry strokes, playing with both hands almost at once.
>
> The abrupt way is also used at a *punctum* or full stop, where the sense is at an end. ([1757] 1974, 47–48)

Because of changes in performance conventions, the avoidance of broken chords in cadences may or may not be applicable to Gasparini's generation. Pasquali's realizations all feature the so-called delayed cadences (ex. 4.17). The V–I progression is played after the singer has finished, while in the original notation the last note in the vocal part coincides with the first cadence chord. The unarpeggiated performance helps to make the ending conclusive (though one may ask if that is always desirable).

Earlier in the century the cadential progression overlapped with the end of the vocal phrase (Hansell 1968) so that the dominant in the V–I progression came with the last words of the recitative (ex. 4.18). In such a context it may well be appropriate to play broken chords in passages of subdued character. (The realization of the dominant chord in the example includes the fourth above the bass, as recommended by Gasparini.)

Gasparini's examples are laid out so they seem to indicate simultaneous broken chords in both hands (ex. 4.19), but that may or may not have been the intention. Pasquali shows all chords as being broken in continuous motion (ex. 4.17) and Gasparini may have the same thing in mind when he says that the chords are played "at a single stroke" ([1708] 1963, 80).

Gasparini's examples show a preponderance of ascending broken chords; a few are descending, and some go in contrary motion. Pasquini frequently breaks the chord down and then up in one sweeping motion, but most often the direction is upward. Gasparini says that after the chord has been played the notes are sustained ([1708] 1963, 79) and Pasquali's examples show that to be the case.

Most of Gasparini's discussion of recitative is concerned with the use of nonharmonic tones. He describes two kinds: mordents, and acciaccaturas. The mordents occur in broken chords and are sounded "a little before the beat and released immediately" ([1708] 1963, 80). Gasparini is quite specific about the non-chord tones suitable for mordents. The half step below the

Example 4.17. N. Pasquali, Continuo Realization of a Recitative

Example 4.18. Undelayed Cadence in Recitative

Example 4.19. F. Gasparini, Acciaccaturas and Voicings in Recitatives

octave from the root works very well in root position and first inversion chords (ex. 4.19a). In root position chords the third may be preceded by the second, but that works best in minor triads (ex. 4.19b).

The acciaccatura is described as from two to four notes close together, usually appearing in rich chords so that the player may have to take two notes with one finger. In example 4.19c the fourth from the bass is described as one of the most common acciaccaturas. At a later time this chord would have been regarded as a second-inversion dominant seventh chord, but that was apparently not a proper chord for Gasparini. His other illustrations show the use of the fourth in dominant seventh chords, particularly in second and third inversions of the chord. In general effect the acciaccatura is apparently not much different from the mordent.

Diminutions in the Accompaniment

One of the most remarkable novelties of Gasparini's *L'armonico pratico* is the discussion of diminutions ([1708] 1963, 85–94). Diminutions and other embellishments "lend grace to the accompaniment" and may be applied to either the treble or the bass part. Diminutions of the bass are used mainly in the ritornelli and consist in breaking up the part into faster motion while maintaining the harmonically important notes in the proper metric position

Example 4.20.   F. Gasparini, Diminutions on the Bass Line

Example 4.21.   F. Gasparini, Diminutions above a Given Bass

(ex. 4.20). When applied to the treble the diminutions no longer consist in breaking up an existing part but in providing a florid treble part. The bass in Gasparini's illustrations generally moves in quarter and eighth notes, while the treble moves in eight and sixteenth notes. The left hand adds a chordal realization suggested by small notes in example 4.21. Gasparini's illustrations show diminutions for various kinds of bass motion: stepwise ascending, stepwise descending, leaps of a third and a fourth. The examples are rather few, and the student is urged to develop taste by listening to good performers.

Taken at face value, Gasparini's diminutions and their purported use by good performers constitute a remarkable invitation for the continuo player to improvise an elaborate accompaniment. That is a complete departure from the ideals of a century earlier when several writers warn against drawing the listener's attention away from the solo part. Gasparini is sometimes misquoted on this issue because he also is concerned about not confusing the singer with diminutions. His concern, however, is narrowly defined, and consists in avoiding intervals and motives that the singer may use ([1708] 1963, 88–89). A florid treble part, in and of itself, is apparently not a source of confusion.

Nothing in the theoretical literature prepares for this complete turnabout in the view of the accompaniment. The change is logical, however, in terms of the stylistic changes in secular vocal music that took place about a generation before Gasparini's book was published in 1708. The monodic style of the early seventeenth century made the vocal part the center of attention and the accompaniment a distinctly subordinate part devoid of musical interest. The basso obbligato aria, which developed in the 1670s, gave the bass melodic independence so that at times it nearly equaled the solo part in importance. The voice was no longer the sole focus of the attention. In principle this development opened the way to greater musical independence in the continuo realization. By 1708 a complete change in the view of the accompaniment had indeed taken place, a view first articulated by Gasparini in *L'armonico pratico*.

Gasparini gives only a few examples of diminutions in the accompaniment, suggesting, however, that he would have liked to give the subject a more extensive treatment. One may perhaps consider Durante's *Partimenti diminuiti* the completion of that task (ex. 4.9). These exercises treat exhaustively a subject only suggested by Gasparini.

If diminutions were improvised on the scale suggested by Gasparini and Durante the accompaniment must have been very elaborate. Arias at that time usually had an obbligato bass so that the harpsichord would have added a third part with melodic and contrapuntal significance. The danger of excess was considerable and it is perhaps likely that the accompaniment sometimes went beyond the boundaries of good taste. J. Bonnet-Bourdelot describes ([1715, 434] MacClintock 1979, 243–44) how the Italian continuo is always ornamented to show off the swiftness of the hand of the players of both the harpsichord and the bass-line instrument. His description, stripped of the element of excess, would fit the basso obbligato aria where the bass instrument has a written-out florid part and where the harpsichord player improvises another.

Bibliography

Dall'Abaco, J. M. C. GB-Lbl MS Add. 31528. *Sonate per violoncello*.

Abraham, G., ed. 1968. *The New Oxford History of Music*. Vol. 4. *The Age of Humanism, 1540–1630*. London: Oxford University Press

Agazzari, A. 1607. *Del sonare sopra il basso con tutti strumenti & uso loro nel concerto*. Siena: Falcini. In Kinkeldey, 1910, *Orgel und Klavier in der Musik des 16. Jahrhunderts*, 216–21.

———. 1608. *Sacrarum Laudum*. Lib. 2.Venice: Amadino. First edition published in 1603.

Albergati Capacelli, P. 1683. *Sonate a due violini col suo basso continuo per l'organo, & un' altro a beneplacito per tiorba, o violoncello*. Opus 2. Bologna: Monti.

———. 1687. *Messa e salmi concertati*. Opus 4. Bologna: Monti.

———. 1691. *Motetti et antifone della B. Vergine*. Opus 7. Bologna: Micheletti.

———. 1702. *Cantate spirituali a una, due, e tre voci con strumenti*. Opus 9. Modena: Rosati.

———. 1714. *Cantate, e oratorii spirituali*. Opus 10. Bologna: Silvani.

———. 1715. *Hinno et antifone della B. Vergine*. Opus 11. Bologna: Silvani.

———. 1721. *Messa, litanie della B.V.* Opus 15. Venice: Bortoli.

Albini, E. 1921. "La viola da gamba in Italia." *Rivista musicale italiana* 28:82.

Arnold, D. 1963. "*L'incoronazione di Poppea* and Its Orchestral Requirement." *The Musical Times* 104:176–78.

———. 1965. "Instruments and Instrumental Teaching in the Early Italian Conservatories." *Galpin Society Journal* 18:72–81.

———. 1966. "Orchestras in Eighteenth-Century Venice." *Galpin Society Journal* 19:3–19.

Arnold, F. T. 1931. *The Art of Accompaniment from a Thorough-Bass, as Practiced in the XVIIth and XVIIIth Centuries*. London: Oxford University Press. Reprint by Dover: New York, 1965.

Aron, P. 1545. *Lucidario in musica di alcune oppenioni antiche, e moderne con le loro oppositioni, e resolutioni*. Venice: Scotto.

Arresti, G. C. 1665. *Sonate a 2, & a tre. Con la parte del violoncello a beneplacito*. Venice: Gardano.

Assandra, C. 1609. *Motetti a due & tre voci, per cantar nell'organo con il basso continuo*. Opus 2. Milan: Tini & Lomazzo.

Bach, C. P. E. 1762. *Versuch über die wahre Art das Clavier zu spielen*. Vol. 2. Berlin. English translation by W. J. Mitchell: *Essay on the True Art of Playing Keyboard Instruments*. New York: Norton, 1949.

Baines, F. 1977. "What Exactly Is a Violone?" *Early Music* 5:173–83.

Banchieri, A. 1595. *Concerti ecclesiastici a otto voci*. Venice: Vincenti.

———. 1607. *Ecclesiastiche sinfonie dette canzoni in aria francese a quattro voci, per sonare, e cantare, & sopra un basso seguente concertare entro organo*. Venice: Amadino.

———. 1609a. *Conclusioni del suono dell'Organo*. Bologna: Rossi. English translation by Lee

Garrett: *Conclusions for Playing the Organ.* Colorado Springs: Colorado College Music Press, 1982.

_____. 1609b. *Gemelli armonici.* Opus 21. Venice: Amadino.

_____. 1611. *L'organo suonarino.* Second edition. Venice: Amadino. First edition 1605, subsequent edition 1628, posthumous edition 1638.

Bassani, G. B. 1683a. *La moralità armonica. Cantate a 2, e 3 voci.* Opus 4. Bologna: Monti.

_____. 1683b. *Sinfonie a due, e tre instromenti.* Opus 5. Bologna: Monti.

_____. 1690. *Armonici entusiasmi di Davide overo salmi concertati a quattro voci con violini e suoi ripieni.* Opus 9. Venice: Sala.

_____. 1691. *Salmi.* Opus 10. Venice: Sala.

_____. 1693. *Armonie festive. O siano motetti sacri a voce sola con violini.* Opus 13. Bologna: Monti.

_____. 1699. *Salmi concertati.* Opus 21. Bologna: Silvani.

_____. 1700. *Le note lugubri concertate ne responsori dell'Ufficio de morti, a quattro voci, con viole, e ripieno.* Opus 23. Venice: Sala.

_____. 1701. *Motetti sacri. A voce sola, con violini.* Opus 27. Bologna: Silvani.

_____. 1704. *Salmi per tutto l'anno a otto voci reali divisi in due cori.* Opus 30. Bologna: Silvani.

_____. 1709. *Acroama missale.* Augsburg: Wagner.

_____. 1710. *Messe concertate.* Opus 32. Bologna: Silvani.

Bellinzani, P. B. 1718. *Salmi brevi per tutto l'anno, a otto voci pieni con violini a beneplacito.* Opus 2. Bologna: Silvani.

Berger, J. 1951. "Notes on Some 17th Century Compositions." *Musical Quarterly* 37:354-67.

Bernabei, D. G. A. 1710. *Sex missarum brevium, cum una pro defunctis, liber 1., a 4. vocibus conc., 4. rip., 2 violinis, 2 violis & violone ad libitum, cum duplici basso continuo.* Augsburg: Wagner.

Bessaraboff, N. 1941. *Ancient European Musical Instruments.* Boston: Harvard University Press.

Bianciardi, F. 1607. *Breve regola per imparar' a sonare sopra il basso con ogni sorte d'istrumento.* Siena: Falcini. See Haas 1929.

Bismantova, B. 1978. *Compendio musicale.* Facsimile edition of MS dated 1677 with additions in 1694. Florence: Studio per Edizione Scelte.

Bonaffino, F. 1623. *Madrigali concertati a due, tre, e quattro voci, per cantar, e sonar nel clavicembalo, chitarrone, o altro simile instrumento.* Messina: Brea.

Bonanni, F. 1723. *Gabinetto armonico.* Rome: Placho.

Bonini, Severo. 1615. *Affetti Spirituali.* Venice: Gardano.

Bonnet-Bourdelot, J. 1715. *Histoire de la musique et de ses effets.* Paris: Cochart. Excerpt in translation in MacClintock 1979.

Bononcini, G. 1686. *Sinfonie a tre instromenti, col basso per l'organo.* Opus 4. Bologna: Monti.

Bononcini, G. M. 1671. *Arie, correnti, sarabande, gighe, & allemande a violino, e violone, over spinetta.* Opus 4. Bologna: Monti.

_____. 1672. *Sonate da chiesa a due violini.* Opus 6. Venice: Gardano.

Bonporti, F. A. 1701. *Motetti a canto solo, con violini.* Opus 3. Venice: Sala.

_____. 1712. *Invenzioni da camera a violino solo con l'accompagnamento d'un violoncello, e cembalo, o liuto.* Opus 10. Bologna: Silvani.

Bonta, S. 1977. "From Violone to Violoncello. A Question of Strings." *Journal of the American Musical Instrument Society* 3:64-99.

_____. 1978. "Terminology for the Bass Violin in Seventeenth-Century Italy." *Journal of the American Musical Instrument Society* 6:5-42.

Bowman, R. 1981. "Musical Information in the Archives of the Church of S. Maria Maggiore, Bergamo, 1649–1720." In *Source Material and the Interpretation of Music. A Memorial Volume to Thurston Dart.* London: Stainer and Bell.

Brown, H. M. 1973. *Sixteenth-Century Instrumentation: The Music for the Florentine Intermedi.* American Institute of Musicology. Studies and Documents 30. Neuhausen-Stuttgart: Hänssler Verlag.

_____. 1976. *Embellishing 16th-Century Music.* London: Oxford University Press.

_____. 1981. Preface to J. Peri, *Euridice.* Recent Researches in the Music of the Baroque Era, 35. Madison, Wisconsin: A-R Editions.

Brunetti, G. 1625. *Salmi intieri concertati a cinque, e sei voci . . . con il basso continuo per sonar nell'organo.* Venice: Vincenti.

Bryden, J. R. 1951. *The Motets of Orazio Benevoli.* Ph.D. diss., The University of Michigan.

Buetens, S. 1969. "The Instructions of Alessandro Piccinini." *Journal of the Lute Society of America, Inc.* 2:6–17.

_____. 1973. "Theorbo Accompaniments of Early Seventeenth-Century Italian Monody." *Journal of the Lute Society of America, Inc.* 6:37–45.

Buonamente, G. B. 1626. *Il quarto libro de varie sonate, sinfonie, gagliarde, corrente, e brandi per sonar con due violini & un basso di viola.* Venice: Vincenti.

_____. 1629. *Il quinto libro de varie sonate, sinfonie, gagliarde, corrente, & ariette per sonar con due violini & un basso di viola.* Venice: Vincenti.

_____. 1637. *Il settimo libro di sonate, sinfonie, gagliarde, correnti, e brandi.* Venice: Vincenti.

Burney, C. 1776–89. *A General History of Music.* 4 vols. London: Printed for the Author.

Caccini, G. 1600. *L'Euridice composta in musica in stile rappresentativo.* Florence: Marescotti.

_____. 1601. *Le nuove musiche.* Florence, Marescotti. English translation in O. Strunk *Source Readings in Music History,* New York: Norton, 1950.

Calvi, L., ed. 1624. *Sacri canti.* Venice: Vincenti.

Capello, G. F. 1612. *Lamentationi, Benedictus, e Miserere da cantarsi il mercordi, giovedi, e venerdi santo di sera a matutino.* Opus 3. Verona: Tamo.

Casa, F. dalla. 1759. I-Bc MS EE.155. *Regole di musica, ed anco le regole per accompagnare sopra la parte per suonare il basso continuo, & per l'arcileuto francese, e per la tiorba.*

Casimiri, R. 1936. "Oratorii del Masini, Bernabei, Melani, di Pio, Pasquini e Stradella, in Roma nell'anno 1675." *Note d'archivio* 13:157–69.

Castaldi, B. 1622. *Capricci a due stromenti, cioè tiorba e tiorbino.* Modena: by the author.

Castello, D. 1621. *Sonate concertate.* Libro primo. Venice: Magni. Subsequent editions in 1629 and 1658. Facsimile edition by Studio per Edizioni Scelte, Florence, 1979.

Cavaliere, G. F. 1634. *Il scolaro principiante di musica.* Naples: Nucci.

Cavalieri, E. de'. 1600. *Rappresentatione di anima e di corpo.* Rome: Mutij. Facsimile edition by D. Alaleoni. Rome: Casa Editrice Claudio Monteverdi, 1912.

Cavalli, F. 1656. *Musiche sacre.* Venice: Vincenti.

Cazzati, M. 1648. *Sonate a una, doi, tre e quattro.* Opus 8. Venice: Vincenti.

_____. 1653. *Messa e Salmi.* Opus 14. Venice: Vincenti.

_____. 1654. *Correnti e balletti.* Opus 15. Venice: Vincenti.

_____. 1656. *Sonate a due violini.* Opus 18. Venice: Magni.

_____. 1659. *Correnti, balletti, gagliarde a 3. e 4 . . . novamente ristampati.* Opus 4. Venice: Magni.

_____. 1660a. *Salmi per tutto l'anno a otto voci brevi, e commodi per cantare con uno, o due organi, e senza ancora se piace.* Opus 21. Bologna: Pisarri.

————. 1660b. *Messa e salmi a tre voci. Alto, tenor, e basso. Con violini, e ripieni a beneplacito.* Opus 24. Bologna: Pisarri.

————. 1663. *Messa e salmi per li defonti a cinque voci con le lettioni, e responsori a 1. 2. 3. con l'aggiunta anco di due violini, e cinque parti di ripieno a beneplacito.* Opus 31. Bologna: Dozza.

————. 1665. *Sonate a due, tre, quattro e cinque, con alcune per tromba.* Opus 35. Bologna: Silvani.

————. 1666. *Messa e salmi a quattro voci con due violini obbligati, e quattro parti di ripieno a beneplacito, con altri salmi a due, e tre voci.* Opus 37. Bologna: Silvani.

Cerone, P. 1613. *El melopeo y maestro.* Naples: Gargano y Nucci.

Cerreto, S. 1601. *Della prattica musica.* Naples: Carlina.

Cesti, A. 1664. A-Wn MS 16890. *Serenata.*

Cherici, S. 1681. *Harmonia di devoti concerti a due e tre voci con violini, e senza.* Opus 2. Bologna: Monti.

Cima, G. P. 1610. *Concerti ecclesiastici . . . & sonate per instrumenti.* Milan: Lomazzo.

Colombi, G. 1673. *La lira armonica.* Opus 2. Bologna: Monti.

————. 1676. *Sonate a due Violini. Con un bassetto viola se piace.* Opus 4. Bologna: Monti.

————. I-Me MS Mus.F. 286. *Toccata a violone solo.*

Colonna, G. P. 1691. *Messa, e salmi concertati.* Opus 10. Bologna: Silvani.

————. 1694. *Psalmi ad vesperas musicis.* Opus 12. Bologna: Silvani.

Cooper, K. and J. Zsako. 1967. "Georg Muffat's Observations on the Lully Style of Performance." *Musical Quarterly* 53:226–45.

Corelli, A. 1681. *Sonate a tre, doi violini, e violone, o arcileuto, col basso per l'organo.* Opus 1. Rome: Mutij.

————. 1689. *Sonate a tre, doi violini, e violone, o arcileuto, col basso per l'organo.* Opus 3. Rome: Komarek.

————. 1700. *Sonate a violino e violone o cimbalo.* Opus 5. Rome: Santa.

Cornetti, P. 1638. *Motetti concertati.* Opus 1. Venice: Vincenti.

Couperin, F. 1714. *Leçons de ténèbres à une et à deux voix.* Paris: Foucault.

Cowling, E. 1975. *The Cello.* New York: Scribner's Sons.

Croce, G. 1594. *Spartitura delli motetti a otto voci.* Venice: Vincenti.

Cross, E. 1981. *The Late Operas of Antonio Vivaldi, 1727-1738.* 2 vols. Studies in British Musicology. Ann Arbor: UMI Research Press.

Degli Antonii, P. 1686. *Suonate a violino solo col basso continuo per l'organo.* Opus 5. Bologna: Monti.

Diruta, A. 1630. *Salmi intieri a quattro voci per il vespero, con il basso per l'organo, se piace.* Opus 12. Rome: Masotti.

Diruta, G. 1609. *Il transilvano.* Vol. 2. Venice: Vincenti.

Dognazzi, F. 1614. *Varii concenti a una et a due voci, per cantar nel chitarone o altri simili istrumenti.* Venice: Gardano.

Doni, G. B. ca. 1635. *Trattato della musica scenica.* In *Trattati di musica.* Florence: Stampa Imperiale, 1763, vol. 1.

————. 1640. *Annotazioni sopra il compendio de' generi, e de' modi della musica.* Rome: Fei.

Donington, R. 1974. *The Interpretation of Early Music.* Second, revised edition. London: Faber.

Dumont, H. 1657. *Meslanges à 2. 3. 4. et 5 parties, avec la basse continue.* Paris: Ballard.

Durante, F. I-Bc MS EE. 171. *Partimenti, ossia intero studio di numerati. Per ben sonare il cembalo.*

————. I-Nc MS Musica didattica 45-1-4. *Partimenti.*

Enrico, E. J. 1976. *The Orchestra at San Petronio in the Baroque Era.* Smithsonian Studies in History and Technology 35. Washington D.C.: Smithsonian Institution.

Fellerer, K. G. 1930. "Das Partimentospiel, eine Aufgabe des Organisten im 18. Jahrhundert." International Musicological Society, *Report of the Congress*, Lüttich.

_____. 1938. "Gebundene Improvisation." *Die Musik* 31:398.

_____. 1940. *Der Partimento-Spieler.* Leipzig: Breitkopf und Härtel.

Fenaroli, F. 18[?] *Metodo nuovamente riformata de' partimenti.* Milan: Ricordi.

Fergusio, G. B. 1612. *Motetti e dialogi per concertar a una sino a nove voci, con il suo basso continuo per l'organo.* Venice: Vincenti.

Fontana, G. B. 1641. *Sonate a 1. 2. 3. per il violino, o cornetto, fagotto, chitarrone, violoncino o simile altro instromento.* Venice: Magni.

Fortune, N. 1953a. *Italian Secular Song from 1600 to 1635.* Ph.D. diss., Cambridge University.

_____. 1953b. "Continuo Instrumentation in Italian Monodies." *Galpin Society Journal* 6:10-13.

Fortune, N., A. Lewis, eds. 1975. *The New Oxford History of Music* Vol. 5: *Opera and Church Music 1630-1750.* London: Oxford University Press.

Franceschini, P. [?] I-Bsp MS p.54.1. *Le Sepulture di Christo.*

Fregiotti, D. I-Nf MS 436. *Oratorio a 3 voci.*

Frescobaldi, G. 1628. *Il primo libro delle canzoni.* Rome: Masotti.

Gaffi, B. 1700. *Cantate da camera a voce sola.* Opus 1. Rome: Mascardi.

Gallerano di Brescia, L. 1629. *Messa e salmi.* Opus 16. Venice: Vincenti.

Ganassi, S. 1543. *Lettione seconda pur della prattica di sonare il violone d'arco.* Venice: n.p.

Gasparini, F. 1695. *Cantate da camera, a voce sola.* Opus 1. Rome: Mascardi.

_____. 1708. *L'armonico pratico al cimbalo.* Venice: Bortoli. English translation by David Burrows: *The Practical Harmonist at the Harpsichord.* New Haven: Yale School of Music, 1963.

Giacobbi, G. 1609. *Prima parte dei salmi concertati a due, e piu chori . . . commodi da concertare in diverse maniere.* Venice: Gardano.

Giustiniani, V. 1878. *Discorso sopra la musica* (1628). Lucca: Giusti. English translation by C. MacClintock. Musicological Studies and Documents 9. Rome: American Institute of Musicology, 1962.

Gmeinwieser, S. 1968. *Girolamo Chiti 1679-1759.* Kölner Beiträge zur Musikforschung 47. Regensburg: Bosse.

_____. 1973. "Die Musikkapellen Roms und ihre Aufführungspraxis unter G. O. Pitoni." *Kirchenmusikalisches Jahrbuch* 57:69-78.

Goldschmidt, H. 1895. "Die Instrumentalbegleitung der italienischen Musikdramen in der ersten Hälfte des XVII. Jahrhunderts." *Monatshefte für Musikgeschichte* 1:53-57.

_____. 1901. *Studien zur Geschichte der italienischen Oper im 17. Jahrhundert.* Leipzig: Breitkopf und Härtel.

Greco, G. I-Mc MS Noseda Z 16-13. *Partimenti.*

_____. I-Nc MS P. 103. *Partimenti.*

Grossi, C. 1675. *L'anfione musiche da camera.* Venice: Gardano.

_____. 1676. *Moderne melodie a voce sola.* Opus 1. Bologna: Monti.

Grove. 1980. *The New Grove Dictionary of Music and Musicians.* Edited by Stanley Sadie. 20 vols. London: Macmillan.

Haas, R. 1929. "Das Generalbassflugblatt Francesco Bianciardis." In *Musikwissenschaftliche Beiträge. Festschrift Johannes Wolf.* Berlin: Breslauer.

Halfpenny, Eric. 1948. "A Note on the Genealogy of the Double Bass." *Galpin Society Journal* 1:41-45.

Hammond, F. 1975. "Musical Instruments at the Medici Court in the Mid-Seventeenth Century." *Analecta Musicologica* 15:202–19.

———. 1979. "G. Frescobaldi and a Decade of Music in Casa Barberini, 1634–1643." *Analecta Musicologica* 19:94–124.

Handel, G. F. 1858–94. *Collected Works.* Leipzig: Breitkopf und Härtel.

Hansell, S. V. 1966. "Orchestral Practice at the Court of Cardinal Pietro Ottoboni." *Journal of the American Musicological Society* 19:398–403.

———. 1968. "The Cadence in 18th-Century Recitative." *Musical Quarterly* 54:229–48.

Hawkins, J. 1776. *A General History of the Science and Practice of Music.* Reprint by Dover, New York, 1963.

Hill, W. H., A. F. Hill, and A. E. Hill. 1902. *Antonio Stradivari.* London: W. E. Hill and Sons.

Horsley, I. 1977. "Full and Short Scores in the Accompaniment of Italian Church Music in the Early Baroque." *Journal of the American Musicological Society* 30:466–99.

I-Bc MS E.25. *Regole di canto figurato, contrappunto, d'accompagnare.*

I-Bc MS P.138. *Regole di canto figurato, e contrapunto et ancora il vero modo di suonare sopra la parte.*

I-Bc MS Q. 45. *D'autori romani, musica volgare.*

d'India, S. 1621. *Le musiche e balli a quattro.* Venice: Vincenti.

Intermedii et concerti, fatti per la comedia rappresentata in Firenze nello nozze del Serenissimo Don Ferdinando Medici, e madama Christina di Lorenzo. Venice: Vincenti, 1591. Modern edition by D. P. Walker: *Musique des Intermedes de "La Pellegrina."* Paris: Editions du Centre National de la Recherche Scientifique, 1963.

I-Rc MS RI. *Regole per accompagnare sopra la parte.*

I-Vnm MS 10269. *Precetti ragionati per apprendere l'accompagnamento del basso sopra gli strumenti da tasto come il gravicembalo, il cembalo, etc.*

Jambe de Fer. 1556. *Epitome musical.* Lyons: M. du Bois.

Jensen, N. M. 1972. "Solo Sonata, Duo Sonata, and Trio Sonata. Some Problems of Terminology and Genre in 17th Century Italian Instrumental Music." *Festskrift J. P. Larsen.* Ed. N. Schiörring, et al. Copenhagen: W. Hansen. 73–101.

———. 1980. "The Performance of Corelli's Chamber Music Reconsidered." In *Nuovissimi studi corellani.* Florence: Olschki.

Jones, A. W. 1982. *The Motets of Carissimi.* 2 vols. Studies in British Musicology 5. Ann Arbor: UMI Research Press.

Joyce, J. J. 1981. *The Monodies of Sigismondo d'India.* Studies in Musicology 47. Ann Arbor: UMI Research Press.

Kapsberger, J. H. 1610. *Villanelle a 1, 2 et 3 voci accommodate per qualsivoglia strumento con l'intavolatura del chitarone.* Rome: n.p.

Keller, W. B. 1958. *The Italian Organ Hymn from Cavazzoni to Arresti.* Ph.D. diss., Harvard University.

Kinkeldey, O. 1910. *Orgel und Klavier in der Musik des 16. Jahrhunderts.* Leipzig: Breitkopf und Härtel.

Kircher, A. 1650. *Musurgia universalis.* Rome: Corbletti.

Kirkendale, U. 1967. "The Ruspoli Documents on Handel." *Journal of the American Musicological Society* 20:222–73.

Klenz, W. 1962. *Giovanni Maria Bononcini.* Durham, North Carolina: Duke University Press.

Kolneder, W. 1970. *A. Vivaldi.* Berkeley: University of California Press.

———. 1973. *Aufführungspraxis bei Vivaldi.* Zürich: Amadeus.

Landshoff, L. 1918. "Uber das vollstimmige Accompagnement und andre Fragen des

Generalbasspiels." In *Festschrift zum 50. Geburtstag Adolf Sandberger.* Munich: Zierfuss. 189–208.

Lanfranco, G. M. 1533. *Scintille di musica.* Brescia: Britannico.

Legrenzi, G. 1663. *Sonate a due, tre, cinque e sei stromenti.* Opus 8. Venice: Magni.

———. 1682. *La cetra. Libro quarto di sonate a due, tre e quattro stromenti.* Opus 10. Venice: Gardano. First edition 1673.

Liess, A. 1957. "Materialen zur römischen Musikgeschichte des seicento." *Acta Musicologica* 29:137–71.

MacClintock, C. 1979. *Readings in the History of Music in Performance.* Bloomington, Indiana: Indiana University Press.

MacDonald, J. A. 1964. *The Sacred Vocal Music of Giovanni Legrenzi.* Ph.D. diss., University of Michigan.

Manfredini, V. 1775. *Regole armoniche o sieno precetti ragionati per apprendere i principi della musica.* Venice: Zerletti.

Marcello, B. 1712. *Suonate a flauto solo con il suo basso continuo per violoncello o cembalo.* Venice: Sala.

———. ca. 1723. *Il teatro all moda.* N.p.: Licante.

———. I-Vnm MS 10752. *Cantate.*

Marini, B. 1626. *Sonate, symphonie, canzoni.* Opus 8. Venice: Gardano.

Marx, K. 1963. *Die Entwicklung des Violoncells und Seinen Spieltechnik bis J. L. Duport (1520-1820).* Regensburg: Bosse.

Mason, K. B. 1983. *The Chitarrone and its Repertoire in Early Seventeenth-Century Italy.* Ph.D. diss., Washington University.

Maugars, A. See MacClintock 1979, 116–26 for translation cited.

Mazzaferrata, G. B. 1674. *Sonate a due violini con un bassetto viola se piace.* Opus 5. Bologna: Monti.

Meyer, E. H. 1946. *English Chamber Music.* London: Lawrence and Wishart.

Micheli, R. 1616. *Compieta a sei voci.* Venice: Vincenti.

Montalbano, F. B. 1629. *Motetti. Ad 1. 2. 3. 4. & 8. voci con il partimento per l'organo.* Palermo: Maringo.

———. 1629. *Sinfonie ad uno, e doi violini, a doi, e trombone, con il partimento per l'organo, con alcune a quattro viole.* Palermo: Maringo.

Monteverdi, C. 1609. *L'Orfeo. Favola in musica. . .rappresentata in Mantova l'anno 1607.* Venice: Amadino.

———. 1638. *Madrigali guerrieri, et amorosi con alcuni opuscoli in genere rappresentativo.* Book 8. Venice: Vincenti.

———. 1926-42. *Tutte le opere.* Ed. G. F. Malipiero. Vienna: Universal.

Musica nova. 1540. Venice: Arrivabene. Modern edition by Colin Slim: Monuments of Renaissance Music 1. Chicago: University of Chicago Press, 1964.

Nenna, P. 1622. *Responsorii di Natale, novamente ristampati, & aggiontovi il partimento per l'organo.* Naples: Beltrano.

Newcomb, A. 1980. *The Madrigal at Ferrara, 1579-97.* 2 vols. Princeton Studies in Music 7. Princeton: Princeton University Press.

Newman, J. 1962. *The Madrigals of Salomon de'Rossi.* Ph.D. diss., Columbia University.

Newman, W. S. 1983. *The Sonata in the Baroque Era.* Third edition. New York: Norton.

Ortiz, D. 1553. *Glose sopra le cadenze, & altre sorte di punti in la musica del violone.* Rome: Dorica.

Pagano, T. I-Nf MS 425. [Various Oratorios.]

———. I-Nf MS 426. [Various Oratorios.]

Panerai, V. C. 1750. *Principij di musica.* Facsimile edition: Kassel: Bärenrieter, 1967.

172   Bibliography

Pasquali, N. 1757. *Thorough-Bass Made Easy.* Facsimile edition. London: Oxford University Press, 1974.

Pasquini, B. GB-Lbl MS Add. 31501/I, II, III. [Keyboard works, including continuo solos.] _____. I-Bc MS D.138. *Regole per bene accompagnare con il Cembalo.*

Pegolotti, T. 1698. *Trattenimenti armonici da camera a violino solo, e violoncello.* Opus 1a. Modena: Rosati.

Penna, L. 1672. *Li primi albori per li principianti della musica figurata.* Bologna: Monti. Other editions: 1679, 1696.

_____. 1678. *Galeria del sacro parnasso.* Bologna: Monti.

Peri, J. 1600. *L'Euridice.* Florence: Marescotti. Modern edition, H. M. Brown: *Euridice.* Madison, Wisconsin: A-R Editions, 1981.

Perti, G. I-Bsp MS P.55.3. *Beata Imelda.*

_____. I-Bsp MS P.57.1. *La Passione di Christo.*

Pesenti, M. 1630. *Correnti alla francese per sonar nel clavicembalo.* Venice: Vincenti.

Piani, G. A. 1712. *Sonate a violino solo e violoncello col cembalo.* Opus 1. Paris: Foucaut.

Piccinini, A. 1623. *Intavolatura di liuto e di chitarrone.* Bologna: Moscatelli.

Plank, S. 1983. "Continuo Realization Fragments from Seventeenth-Century Rome." *The Courant* 1:11–18.

Planyavsky, A. 1970. *Geschichte des Kontrabasses.* Tutzing: Schneider.

Po, G. M. I-Ac MS N.169/1. *Adducentur Regi virgines, offertorio a 2.*

_____. I-Ac MS N.183/8 *Adorabo a 2.*

Porpora, N. A. 1754. *Sonate XII di violino, e basso.* Vienna: Bernardi.

Porta, E. 1620. *Sacro convito musicale ornato di varie, et diverse vivande spirituali a una, due, tre, quattro, cinque, & sei voci.* Opus 7. Venice: Vincenti.

Praetorius, M. 1619a. *Polyhymnia caduceatrix & panegyrica.* In the *Collected Works,* vol. 17. Wolfenbüttel: Kallmeyer, 1930.

_____. 1619b. *Syntagma musicum.* Vol. 2: *De Organographia.* Vol. 3: *Termini musici.* Wolfenbüttel: Holwein. Facsimile edition, Kassel: Bärenreiter, 1958–59.

Prandi, G. I-Bc MS E.19. *Compendio della musica.*

Puliaschi, G. D. 1618. *Musiche varie.* Rome: Zanetti.

Purcell, H. 1697. *Ten Sonatas in Four Parts.* London: Heptinstall.

Quantz, J. J. 1752. *Versuch einer Anweisung die Flöte traversiere zu spielen.* Berlin: Vos. Facsimile edition, Kassel: Bärenreiter, 1953. English translation by E. R. Reilly: *On Playing The Flute.* New York: Schirmer, 1966.

Reese, G. 1959. *Music in the Renaissance.* Revised edition. New York: Norton.

Rose, G. 1965. "Agazzari and the Improvising Orchestra." *Journal of the American Musicological Society* 18:382–93.

Rossi, S. de'. 1607. *Il primo libro delle sinfonie et gagliarde a tre, quattro, e a cinque voci.* Venice: Amadino.

_____. 1613. *Il terzo libro de varie sonate, sinfonie, gagliarde, brandi, e corrente.* Venice: Vincenti.

Rovetta, G. 1639. *Messa, e salmi concertati a cinque, sei, sette, otto voci, e due violini.* Opus 4. Venice: Vincenti.

Sadie, J. 1980. *The Bass Viol in French Baroque Chamber Music.* Ann Arbor: UMI Research Press.

Sartori, C. 1952. *Bibliografia della musica strumentale italiana stampata in Italia fino al 1700.* Florence: Olschki.

_____. 1962. *La Cappella della Basilica di S. Francesco. Biblioteca. Catalogo del fondo musicale nella Biblioteca Comunale di Assisi.* Milan: Istituto Editoriale Italiano.

Scarlatti, A. I-Nc MS 33.3.17. *Le nozze col nemico.*

_____. GB-Lbl MS Add. 14244. *Regole per principianti.*

_____. GB-Lbl MS Add. 16126. *Il prigioner fortunato.*

_____. I-Nc MS 34.5.2. *Da sventura a sventura.*

Schneider, M. 1918. *Die Anfänge des Basso Continuo.* Leipzig: Breitkopf und Härtel.

Schnoebelen, A. 1969. "Performance Practices at San Petronio in the Baroque." *Acta Musicologica* 41:37–55.

Selfridge-Field, E. 1975. *Venetian Instrumental Music from Gabrieli to Vivaldi.* New York: Praeger.

Silvani, G. A. 1720. *Messe brevi a quattro voci piene.* Opus 11. Bologna: Silvani.

_____. 1724. *Versi della turba per il Passii della Domenica delle Palme, e Venerdi Santo.* Opus 12. Bologna: Silvani.

_____. 1725. *Litanie della Beata Vergine a quattro voci concertate con violini, e ripieni.* Opus 14. Bologna: Silvani.

Sites, C. 1959. *Benedetto Marcello's Chamber Cantatas.* Ph.D. diss., University of North Carolina, 1959.

Slim, C. 1964. See *Musica nova* 1540.

Smith, D. A. 1979. "On the Origin of the Chitarrone." *Journal of the American Musicological Society* 32:440–62.

Spencer, R. 1976. "Chitarrone, Theorbo, Archlute." *Early Music* 4:408–22.

Stradella, A. I-Bc MS BB361. *San Giovanni Battista.*

_____. I-Vnm MS 99. *Cantatas.*

Strunk, O. 1950. *Source Readings in Music History.* New York: Norton.

Taglietti, G. 1707. *Pensieri musicali a violino, e violoncello col basso continuo a parte all'uso d'arie cantabili.* Opus 6. Venice: Bortoli.

Tevo, Z. 1705. *Il musico testore.* Venice: Bortoli.

Thoinan, E. 1865. *Maugars.* Paris: Claudin. Reprint by Baron, London, 1965.

Tonini, B. 1697. *Suonate da chiesa a tre, due violini & organo, con violoncello ad libitum.* Opus 2. Venice: Sala.

Torelli, G. 1686. *Sonate a tre stromenti con il basso continuo.* Opus 1. Bologna: Micheletti.

_____. 1692. *Sinfonie a tre, e concerti a quattro.* Opus 5. Bologna: Micheletti.

Trabaci, G. M. 1605. *Missarum, et motectorum quatuor vocum, cum partimento pro organista.* Book 1. Naples: Vitale.

_____. 1634. *Passionem D. N. Jesu Christe.* Naples: Beltranum.

Troilo, A. 1606. *Canzoni da sonare.* Venice: Amadino.

Turini, F. 1629. *Madrigali a cinque, cioè tre voci, e due violini con un basso continuo duplicato per un chitarrone o simil istromento.* Venice: Vincenti.

Uccelini, M. 1642. *Sonate, arie, et correnti a 2, e 3.* Venice: Vincenti.

Valle, P. della. ca. 1640. *Della Musica dell'eta nostra.* In G. B. Doni, *Trattati di Musica.* Florence: Stampa Imperiale, 1763, vol. 2.

Vatielli, F. 1927. *Arte e vita musicale a Bologna.* Bologna: Zanichelli.

Viadana, L. G. da. 1602. *Cento concerti ecclesiastici.* Venice: Vincenti.

Vitali, F. 1641. *Psalmi ad Vesperas quinque vocibus cum basso ad organum si placet.* Rome: Bianchi.

Vitali, G. B. 1667. *Sonate a due violini col suo basso continuo per l'organo.* Bologna: Monti.

Vocabulario degli Accademici della Crusca. 1729. Fourth edition. Florence: Manni.

Walker, D. P. 1963. *Musique des Intermèdes de "La Pellegrina."* Paris: Editions du Centre National de la Recherche Scientifique.

Walther, J. 1732. *Musikalisches Lexikon.* Facsimile edition by R. Schaal. Kassel: Bärenreiter, 1953.

Wellesz, E. 1913–14. "Zwei Studien zur Geschichte der Oper im XVII. Jahrhundert." *Sammelbände I.M.G.* Vol. 15. Leipzig: Breitkopf und Härtel.

Wessely Kropik, H. 1961. *Lelio Colista.* Vienna: Boehlhaus.

Williams, P. 1969. "Basso Continuo on the Organ." *Music and Letters* 50:136–52, 230–45.

——. 1970. *Figured Bass Accompaniment.* Edinburgh: Edinburgh University Press.

Zacconi, L. 1596. *Prattica musica.* Venice: Carampello. First edition, 1592.

Zannetti, G. 1645. *Il scolaro . . . per imparar a suonare di violin, et altri stromenti.* Milan: Camagno.

Index

Acciaccatura: Gasparini on, 159, 161

Accompaniment: keyboard and cello, 5; according to published parts, 17; provided by the singer, 18; from a score or improvised, 16–17; sixteenth-century, 14–15, 18; terms for, 12–14; in vocal solos, according to Caccini, 17–18. *See also* Basso continuo

Agazzari, A., *Del sonare sopra il basso...* (1607): bass-line doubling, 6; improvisation, 124; lutes, 111–12; the organist, 16; ornamenting vs. foundation instruments, 12, 124–25; passaggi, 130; related to sacred music, 125; texture, 128; voice-leading, 129; written-out realization, 127

Albergati, Capacelli, *Messa...* (1721): parts for bass-line instruments in, 49

Archlute
—description: general, 1, 93–94; changes after 1680, 94, 98–99
—use: by L. Baroni, 38; in arpeggiated realizations, 113, 116; according to Cavalli, 6; in church sonatas, 1; contrasted with use of theorbo, 97; according to Gasparini, 42; in oratorios, 34–35; reappearance, late seventeenth century, 106–7; at Rome, 46
—tuning, 94

Arpeggio: in recitative accompaniments, 158–61

Arresti, G. C., *Sonate a 2 & a tre:* doubling of parts in, 30

Assandra, C., *Motetti...* (1609): first mention of violone, 76

Assisi, Basilica of Saint Francis, catalog of sacred music, 1600–1800: bass parts listed in, 50

Bach, C. P. E., *Versuch über die wahre Art das Clavier zu spielen:* on doubling the bass line, 5–6

Banchieri, Adriano
—*Conclusioni del suono dell' organo* (1609): on scores for the accompanist, 17; on the violone, 72, 83–84
—*Ecclesiastiche sinfonie:* on terminology for accompaniments, 12, 15
—*Gemelli armonici:* on terminology for accompaniments, 13
—*L'organo suonarino:* on continuo solos, 130–31; *Dialogo musicale* on realizing a basso continuo, 134; on the violin family, 83–84

Baroni, Adriana: as a self-accompanied singer, 38

Baroni, Leonora: as a self-accompanied singer, 38

Baschenis, Evaristo: painter of a work depicting a bass gamba, 78

Bass, fast motion in: realization, 130

Bassani, G. B.: *Salmi...* (1704), bass-line instruments in, 49; *Sinfonie...* (1683), bass parts in, 26, 28

Bassetti: defined, 17, 130

Bassetto (di viola): small bass violin, 83, 84–85

Bass gamba: tuning, 71, 87

Bass line: in operatic arias, ca. 1670, 39–41

Bass-line doubling: after 1680, 63–64; in church sonatas, 28; documentation for, 8, 9; in Gasparini's solo cantatas, 42–43; in large ensembles, 66; in late seventeenth-century orchestral practice, 30; in opera, 31–34, 62–63; in oratorio, 34–35; rationale for, 5–9; in sacred vocal music, 45–50; whether indicated by number of parts, 9, 21

Bass-line instruments: after 1680, 63–64; early baroque performance, 62–63; interchangeability, 106–7; parts for, 5, 9, 41–42, 50; in sacred vocal music, 45–50; terminology, according to Cazzati, 75–76

Basso: term for chordal instrument, 13

Maugars, André: on performance practice in Rome (1639), 38, 46, 77, 112
Mazzaferrata, G. B., *Sonata a due violini...* (1674): optional bass parts in, 28
Monody, seventeenth-century: doubling the bass line in, 37–38
Monteverdi, Claudio: *Il combattimento di Tancredi e Clorinda,* instruments used in, 33, 37, 73; dramatic vs. vocal ensemble works, basso continuo in, 37; *Orfeo,* instrumental accompaniment in, 32–33
Musica nova: organ accompaniment first mentioned in, 15

Naldi, Antonio: inventor of chitarrone, 94
Naples: continuo practice (partimenti), 141–47; Oratorio dei Filippini, performing parts at, 34

Opera: bass-line doubling in, 31–34, 62–63, 66
Oratorio: bass-line doubling in, 34–35
Orchestra, seventeenth-century, 28–30, 39, 48
Organ: use, in the church sonata, 24, 28; doubling voice parts, 17; in opera, 33; in oratorio, 34; use according to various writers, 6, 15–16, 19, 46, 61–62
Organist, role of, 7, 14, 16
Organo di legno: in Monteverdi's *Orfeo,* 32
Organo suave: in *Eurydice,* 32
Ornamenting instruments: Agazzari on, 11–12, 112–13, 124–25
Ortiz, Diego, *Tratado de glosas:* accompaniments in, 14–15
Ostinato: in seventeenth-century arias, 40–41

Pagano, Thomas, *La morte di Maria Magdalena:* bass part in, 34
Partidura, 12
Partimento (pl. *partimenti*)
—as accompaniment, 12, 14, 123, 141
—as continuo solos, 141–47; fugal partimenti, 145–46; manuals, 141–45, 146–47; partimenti diminuiti, 144–45
Partitio, 12, 14
Partitione, 13, 14
Partitura, 14
Pasquali, N., *Thorough-Bass Made Easy* (1757): on arpeggios in recitative accompaniments, 158, 159–60; texture, 157; voice leading, 158
Pasquini, B.: continuo solos, 131–32
Payment records: use for determining performance practice, 8–9
Pegolotti, T., *Trattenimenti armonici da camera...* (1698): performance of bass part, 57

Penna, L., *Li primi albori musicale...* (1672): basso continuo, construction of, 65; basso continuo realization (after 1650), 136–37
Performance parts, original: use for determining performance practice, 9
Peri, J.: *Eurydice,* instruments in, 32; as a performer in the Florentine *Intermedii,* 31
Pesenti, Martino, *Correnti alla francese...* (1630): trio texture in, 52, 53
Piani, G. A., *Sonate a violino solo...* (1712): performance of bass part, 58
Piccinini, Alessandro, *Intavolatura di liuto...* (1623): archlute, inventor of, 93–94; chitarrone, arpeggiation on, 98; extended lutes, use of, 109
Plucked instruments: use for accompaniments, 38; vs. sustaining instruments, 32. *See also* Archlute; Chitarrone; Extended lutes
Polychoral works: basso continuo parts for, 16
Porpora, N.A., *Sonate XII di violino e basso:* performance of bass part in, 59
Praetorius, Michael
—*Polyhymnia caduceatrix & panegyrica:* on instrumental doubling of voice parts, 8
—*Syntagma musicum* (1619): bass-line doubling, 7–8; bass-line instruments, 6, 102; small bass violin, tuning, 83
Prandi, G., *Compendio della musica* (1606): violone, tuning and fingering of, 71
Precetti ragionati: bogus treatise on basso continuo, 123, 138–40
Purcell, Henry, *Ten Sonatas in Four Parts:* basso continuo in, 62

Quantz, Johann, J.: on use of violone and cello, 79

Recitative: accompaniments for, 158–61
Regole...d'accompagnare: on realizing a basso continuo, 134–35; on realizing an unfigured bass, 135
Ricci, Agostino: use of bass-line instruments, 50
Rome, seventeenth-century sacred music at: bass-line doubling, 45–46
Rossi, Salomon de', instrumental works: performance of bass parts in, 52–53, 105

Sacred vocal music: bass-line doubling in, 45–50; bass-line instruments in, 106–7; basso continuo parts in, 16–17; monody, basso continuo parts in, 18–19; sixteenth-century, instruments used in, 16
Scarlatti, Alessandro, *Le nozze col nemico:* aria "in the lute style," 113, 115